American Dreams

"What's the matter with you?" Meg spat at Luke, tears filling her eyes no matter how hard she tried not to let it happen. "Are you *trying* to break up Drew and me?"

Luke paused a long moment, looking a little stunned at her outburst. He adjusted his glasses and spoke very quietly. "You know what I always liked about you, Meg? That you always liked to look deeper into things, to not just take them at face value."

Meg reeled from Luke's words, as well as from what was written on the pages he'd given her. She didn't know how to respond to any of it. So, instead, she merely walked to the door of the Vinyl Crocodile, as though she were in a trance.

"Meg," Luke called out to her.

Meg couldn't look back at him, just put her hand on the doorknob and waited.

"Are you ever planning on coming back in here?"

Meg thought about her answer to that question a long time. When she finally spoke, it wasn't much more than a whisper. "I'm not sure."

American Dreams

COUNT ON ME

by Adam Beechen

SIMON SPOTLIGHT ENTERTAINMENT

New York   London   Toronto   Sydney

This book is a work of fiction. Any references to historical events, real people, or real locales are used fictitiously. Other names, characters, places, and incidents are the product of the author's imagination, and any resemblance to actual events or locales or persons, living or dead, is entirely coincidental.

Simon Spotlight Entertainment
An imprint of Simon & Schuster Children's Publishing Division
1230 Avenue of the Americas, New York, New York 10020
© 2004 NBC Studios—Universal Television
SIMON SPOTLIGHT ENTERTAINMENT and colophon are registered trademarks of Simon & Schuster, Inc.
Manufactured in the United States of America
First Edition 10 9 8 7 6 5 4 3 2 1
ISBN 0-689-87170-8
Library of Congress Control Number: 2004102539

For my mother, Judy Beechen, who still loves the music.

COUNT ON ME

One

The bells over the Vinyl Crocodile's door jangled musically as Meg Pryor walked in, leaving the crisp late September air behind. The Saturday sky outside was as gray as lead, and everyone seemed to be wearing heavy coats of the same drab color. Meg could feel winter in the air, and soon there would be snow, turning the streets white for a few hours, then dirty gray.

A trumpet blared over the record store's hi-fi, and thanks to her ex-boyfriend Luke Foley's informal music appreciation lessons, Meg could tell that she was listening to Dave Brubeck. Meg had never liked jazz or folk music, Luke's two greatest musical passions, before she met Luke—or, more accurately, she hadn't known anything about jazz or folk before he told her about them. But now, through the records he had given her, as well as the discussions they'd had after she'd listened to them, Meg found it all interesting, if not the kind of music she'd rush out and buy. Just from hearing the music on the stereo in the store, Meg knew instantly that Mr. Greenwood, who owned the store and employed both Luke and Meg's best friend, Roxanne Bojarski, wasn't in. Mr. Greenwood never let Luke play jazz or folk when he was around. "That's not what the customers want," he'd yell. "They want to buy rock and roll, so let them hear rock and roll!" Luke would roll his eyes behind his thick Buddy Holly–style glasses, tug at his unruly dark hair, and nod. Then, the minute Mr. Greenwood would step out, the needle would come off Manfred Mann's "Do Wah Diddy Diddy" record, or some other rock tune that was burning up the charts in 1964, and the cool piano of Thelonious Monk would fill the store.

Meg paused at the door, taking in the whole of the record shop. She knew every inch of it. She could list what was in the racks practically by heart. The smell of the cardboard record jackets and the paper sleeves around the vinyl was as familiar to her as her father's aftershave.

Luke stood behind the counter, peering intently through his glasses at a bunch of papers spread out before him. He was cute, there was no doubt about it. And there'd been a time when all Luke had to do was look at her out of the corner of his eye, a knowing glance just between them, that made her feel like some special and private unspoken communication had passed between them, something only the two of them could understand. Butterflies would tickle her stomach, and her knees would go a little weak. Once upon a time.

Meg walked over to him, and leaned over the counter, twisting her body so she could look up into his eyes. "Hi there," she said. "What's the style at the Crocodile?"

"I'll tell you in a while, I've got it on file," Luke rhymed back, as was their custom, his voice flat.

Familiar patterns. From the weather outside, to the Vinyl Crocodile and its music, sights, and smells, to the way she and Luke said hello. Meg sighed, and turned around to face the store, leaning back on the counter. She'd spent all sixteen of her years in Philadelphia, and it felt like some parts of her life never, ever changed.

What about Drew? she reminded herself.

Meg had to smile at this thought. Drew was a big change in her life, and a good one. She had never dated anybody like Drew Mandel before. She hadn't dated many people *before* Drew—just her former dance partner at *American Bandstand,* Jimmy Riley, kind of, sort of, and then Luke.

Why her relationship with Luke had ended was

still something of a mystery to Meg. They had simply seemed to be moving further and further apart from each other. It was as if they had been standing side-by-side, then the floor slowly started to move under their feet, forcing Meg one way and Luke the other. And when she finally noticed it happening, they were miles apart. They had stopped dating, but it had been a surprisingly easy break-up. Her idea of break-ups had been shaped by teen magazines, movies, and stories told to her by Roxanne. They almost always involved someone being furious with someone else, lots of dramatic yelling and tears, and a long period afterward spent in bed, unable to face the outside world. But for both Meg and Luke, breaking up just seemed the right thing to do, and there was no drama involved.

With her social schedule newly open, Meg had begun spending more time at Penn with her older brother JJ's fiancée, Beth. Meg adored Beth. She was bright, caring, smart, and independent—in many ways, exactly what Meg hoped to be. Drew lived in the same dormitory as Beth, and gradually Meg found herself spending less time with Beth, and more time with Drew. She had seen him speak at a free speech rally recently, and was very impressed by his commitment to changing the world. Having watched students at other schools organize to protest wrongs in the community or at their universities, Drew had become a driving force in trying to do the same things at Penn.

He had also kissed Meg, just a few times so far, but enough to make her want to be around him even more. As good a speaker as Drew was, it was possible he was an even better kisser.

"Meg?" Luke asked from behind her. "You okay?"

It took some effort to push aside her happy thoughts of Drew, but Meg managed to do so. She turned to face Luke, who was still studying his papers. "Sure," Meg answered, and took one of the papers to look at for herself. "What are you doing?"

Luke sighed, and reached under his glasses to rub his eyes. "Monday is New Release Day . . . a whole batch of new forty-fives," he told her. "That means today is Paperwork Day. I've got to double and triple check all the orders." He sighed. "It always seems to happen on a day that both Roxanne and Mr. Greenwood have off. I think it's a conspiracy."

Something on the list caught Meg's eye. "The Supremes?" she gasped excitedly. "The Supremes have a new single coming out tomorrow?"

"Don't get your hopes up," Luke warned. "I

talked to the distributor in New York. He's listened to it, and says it's not one of their best."

"I bet you're wrong," Meg challenged him playfully. Holding the paper, she moved away from the counter. "The song is called, 'I'm Waving Goodbye.' That's a great title!"

Moving her hips side to side, her feet to a dance rhythm, Meg backed toward the door, waving with her free hand. "Even though right now I'm here with you," she sang to a made-up tune, "in my heart I'm waving good-bye . . ."

"It's got a good beat, and you can dance to it," Luke said, copying the kind of review kids might give on *American Bandstand*. "I give it an eighty-three."

Meg put her hands on her hips in mock exasperation. "An eighty-three," she scolded. "It's much better than that!"

Luke tapped a pen against his chin and looked to the ceiling, seeming to rethink his position. "Well, maybe you're right. Eighty-four."

Meg took a bow. "That's more like it. Thank you, thank you!"

Luke leaned both elbows on the counter. "You're sure in a good mood today," he said. "What's up?"

Meg thought for a moment about how to answer

the question. Should she just blurt out her excitement about Drew? Part of her wanted to, but another, louder part of her thought perhaps she should keep Drew to herself a little while longer. Meg felt she and Drew were headed in a good direction, and the last thing she wanted to do was jinx that. "I'm heading up to Penn after today's *Bandstand*," she said instead. "My family's putting together a care package for JJ, and Beth is sending some things along, too."

"How's JJ doing?" Luke asked, concern in his voice.

"Fine, I think," Meg told Luke. "We don't hear from him as much as we'd like." JJ had enlisted in the marines and moved to Camp Lejeune for basic training. He had joined in hopes of advancing his dreams of becoming an astronaut, but it still scared Meg a little, knowing that JJ might be headed for Viet Nam, and maybe combat. Viet Nam, though it had been on everyone's lips for a long time, still sounded impossibly foreign to Meg, impossibly far away. She was barely able to find it on a map, let alone consider the possibility of her brother actually having to go there.

Luke nodded. "Well, I'm sure he'd love to get something from home," he said. "I should see if I can talk Mr. Greenwood into letting me send along some freebie records, to help out our boys in uniform and all that. You know, I think it's terrific that you're spending so much time with Beth, especially with JJ away at boot camp."

Meg felt a tiny touch of guilt that she hadn't told Luke the whole truth, just part of it. "Yeah, Beth's great," Meg said.

A little of Meg's inner emotions must have shown on Meg's face, because Luke cocked his head to one side and looked at her curiously. "Is something else going on?"

Meg shrugged. "No," she said. "Why?"

Now Luke shrugged. "Just a feeling I'm getting," he told her. "Is everything going all right at *Bandstand*?"

"Oh, yeah, yeah," she assured him. "*Bandstand's* great."

The door to one of the two listening booths at the back of the store opened, and Sam Walker stepped out, carrying a small stack of 45s. He looked up at Meg with some surprise. They hadn't seen much of each other since the previous summer, when she'd been caught out in the awful rioting that rampaged through her city after the deaths of three civil rights activists in Mississippi. She hadn't meant to be out when the rioting started—heck, it wasn't like she *knew* there was going to be a riot! She had just been on her way to see Sam, who worked at her father's store, Pryor TV and Radio, and the next thing she knew, Philadelphia was going crazy all around her, with black people damaging and looting white-owned stores, and threatening whites with bodily harm. Sam, who was black, did his best to protect Meg when violence broke out, but if not for the timely arrival of her uncle Pete, a policeman, who knew what might have happened?

Though they were friends, the riots had reminded Meg and Sam how different they were from each other, and their conversations had become fewer and farther between. It had become strange to be around Sam, like she didn't know exactly how to behave or talk to him. Meg still felt bad that she hadn't been there enough for Sam in the days before his mother's recent death. Sam seemed to understand, but things were still a little . . . off. Meg supposed they would eventually get back to normal, but it would probably take some time.

"Hi, Sam," she managed.

"Hi," he replied. "What's going on?"

Luke looked at Sam and jerked a thumb in Meg's

direction. "Meg's going up to Penn later to see her brother's fiancée, but I think she's got other plans, too."

Sam raised an eyebrow. "Oh yeah? Like what?"

Meg laughed nervously. "Nothing! I'm telling you guys, I'm going to see Beth!"

Luke leaned forward again, impatiently awaiting details. "Aaaaaaand . . . ?"

Meg looked to Sam for help, but he only half-smiled and folded his arms, leaving her on her own.

Meg looked down at the floor and shuffled her feet, absently moving them through a dance step out of reflex as her hands folded and refolded Luke's piece of paper. She couldn't help smiling, and could feel her cheeks begin to blush. The part of her that wanted to talk about Drew grew much louder than the part telling her not to jinx it. "Well," she said quietly, "there's kind of this guy."

Luke suddenly stood up straight, as though he'd been poked in the back with something sharp. He started to say something, then closed his mouth so abruptly Meg actually heard his teeth clack together. But he blinked a few times, and smiled a weird smile. "What, a guy like a *guy*?" he asked. "Like a *dating* kind of guy?"

Again, Meg looked at Sam. He still had his arms folded, and he still smiled his sort-of-smile. Meg couldn't tell what he was thinking, but could tell that he wasn't about to bail her out by changing the conversation, even if she wanted him to.

"He's one of Beth's friends," Meg said, turning back to Luke.

"A college guy," Luke responded.

Meg nodded. "He's . . . interesting," she went on. "He's smart—*so* smart—and he wants to know everything about everything! And he's funny, and he really wants to make the world a better place. And when you listen to him, you think he can do it, that he *will* do it!" Meg was about to go on and tell them about some of the other qualities that made Drew interesting to her—like his perfect smile and brown eyes, but decided against it. She didn't want to sound silly about him.

"He sounds like Superman," Luke said with a funny-sounding voice. Like he was maybe trying to tease Meg about Drew, but it was getting caught somewhere in his throat. "What's his name?"

"Drew," Meg told him. "Drew Mandel." She liked saying it.

Sam nodded. He looked from Luke, who was wearing a stone-faced expression, and back to Meg. "So he *is* a dating kind of guy," he said.

Meg couldn't answer. But she could feel color

rising to her cheeks as she blushed once more and looked at the floor again.

"That's great, Meg," Luke said, that strange tightness still in his voice. "Sounds like a cool guy. I'm happy for you."

She looked up at him and smiled. "Yeah," she said, "I'm really happy too." She saw the clock above the counter and gasped. "I'm also really late to get to the station for *Bandstand*!" She put Luke's piece of paper back in front of him and did her little dance step back toward the door, lifting her hand to Luke and Sam.

"In my heart, I'm waving good-bye," she sang. The bells jingled again as the door closed behind her.

Two

"**O**ver here! Over here!"

"Me next! Me!"

"Sign this!"

"Can you get me in?"

It was half an hour before *American Bandstand* was to go on the air, and Meg had arrived just in time to meet Roxanne for the dancers' last few minutes on Autograph Row. That was what the Regulars, *Bandstand*'s steady group of dancers, called the small strip of sidewalk just outside the WFIL studio on 46th and Market. It was where fans of the show stood behind ropes, hoping for a glimpse of their favorite Regulars, or to be selected by the Line Guy to dance with the Regulars on that day's show.

Looking at all the kids standing three deep behind the ropes, Meg marveled. *It wasn't so long ago that I was standing where they are,* she thought. *Just a few feet away.* For months, she and Roxanne had been fixtures on Autograph Row, trying desperately to be noticed.

She remembered what it had been like, on the other side of those ropes, hoping for a look, a moment of contact with someone whose face she had seen on television, maybe even a quick exchange with Jimmy Riley, her favorite Regular. And most of all, she wanted the chance to dance with all of them, a chance to be on the television herself. Her father, of course, hadn't understood. "Isn't there a better way for you to be spending your time than waiting in a line all afternoon?" he'd say. Meg thought it was funny that a man who made his living selling televisions couldn't understand why his daughter wanted to be *on* television so badly. And when she got her chance, when Roxanne's sneaky maneuverings got them the opportunity to step inside WFIL's doors, Meg had to fight her father tooth and nail to get him to agree to let her be on the show. It was a constant struggle. Meg felt that any poor grade, any backtalk, any little slip-up might result in the "privilege," as her dad called it, of being allowed to dance on *Bandstand* to be taken away.

But so far, Meg had kept up her end of that bargain, and now all those kids were looking at *her.*

Wasn't that amazing? Though Meg generally felt the furthest thing from being a star, it tickled her to think that some young boy or girl would go home, look at the little slip of paper she'd signed, and think, *I got the autograph of someone who dances on* Bandstand. And then she would laugh out loud. *Don't they know I'm just Meg Pryor?* Meg loved signing autographs, and she was sincerely grateful for every one.

Roxanne signed every autograph with a flourish, occasionally with a flirty message if she was signing for a boy. "To David from Roxanne," she'd write. "Keep smiling that gorgeous smile!" She loved the attention, soaking it up like a flower soaks up water.

Meg hurried over to join Roxanne on Autograph Row. "Sorry I'm late," she said, out of breath. "I stopped in at Vinyl Crocodile and lost track of time."

Roxanne chuckled, handing a slip of paper back to a star-struck boy a year or two younger than they were. "Is Luke going crazy with Paperwork Day?"

Meg reached out and grabbed a pen and paper from a sea of imploring arms and outstretched hands. "He says he is, but I think he secretly loves it. He loves organizing things, finishing projects, stuff like that." She handed the paper and pen back.

"Thanks," she called into the crowd, unsure of exactly which hand belonged to her autograph-seeker. "Keep watching!" She reached for another pen.

"Hmm," Roxanne said, deep in thought.

Meg glanced over at her. "What?"

Rox shrugged. "Nothing. It's just, for someone who's not dating Luke anymore, you sure spend a lot of time with him."

"I do not," Meg replied defensively. "He just happens to work at my favorite record store, and I happen to go there a lot. And besides, we're friends."

"And besides that, there's Drew," Roxanne pointed out.

"Yeah," Meg agreed, then thought about it for a second. "Well, no. I don't know. I'm not sure what Drew and I are, but that doesn't have anything to do with my friendship with Luke."

Roxanne raised an eyebrow. "Oh no?"

Suddenly, a pimply-faced boy leaned out of the crowd across the rope, grinning hopefully and dreamily at Meg. "Excuse me, will you be my first kiss?" he begged, his voice breaking.

Meg took a step back, surprised, and looked at the boy, both uneasily and sympathetically. "I can't," she told him. "I've got a . . ." She paused, suddenly unable to complete the sentence.

Roxanne leaned over helpfully. "She's got a Drew," she finished for Meg.

The boy frowned, confused and disappointed, and retreated back into the crowd. Meg looked at Roxanne, who shrugged again. The two girls went back to signing autographs.

After a moment, someone behind them said, "Are you Roxanne Bojarski?"

Meg and Roxanne turned around to find a very pretty girl, who was a year or two older than they were, with blond hair shorter than Meg's, a slim figure accentuated by a skirt that was short enough to rival Roxanne's, and what looked like a very expensive blouse. Her smile was bright and perfect.

Roxanne looked her up and down. "That's me," she said.

"I'm Sherry Mann," the girl said, holding out her hand. Roxanne shook it tentatively. "I'm one of the new production assistants on the show."

"Oh," Roxanne said, puzzled.

"I was just talking to Lenny Beeber," Sherry went on, still smiling. "He said you were his girlfriend."

Roxanne again looked Sherry over, and dropped her hand suspiciously. "That's right."

Lenny was also a production assistant on *American Bandstand,* where both Meg and Rox danced, and the bassist for a hopeful new rock band called Lenny and the Pilgrims. While the band may not have been as good as the Rolling Stones, Meg thought they were very good, and could see a day when she and Rox might be dancing to music by Lenny and his friends on *Bandstand.*

Sherry nodded. "Well, I just thought I'd come over and introduce myself, since I'm new around here and I don't know anyone. Also, the show's associate producer . . . I forget his name . . ."

"Colin," Meg said helpfully, then added, "I'm Meg," earning her a glare from Roxanne.

"Hi, Meg. That's right: Colin. Colin said it's time for everyone to come in."

"Okay," Rox responded. "Thanks."

Sherry waved cheerfully and walked back into the television studio. Roxanne stared after her. "She seemed nice," Meg ventured.

"*Seemed* is the right word," Roxanne said, her dark eyes darkening even further.

From where she sat in the bleachers, Meg looked up at the bright lights above the *Bandstand* stage, trying to summon a sneeze. Her younger sister, Patty, had told her that lights somehow affected the nasal passages when you needed to sneeze, making it easier when you felt that annoying tickle in your nose. Patty was often a brainy, know-it-all brat, Meg thought, but once in a while, she had some useful information. Not that Meg would ever give Patty the satisfaction of telling her that.

Meg felt her eyes water and squeeze shut as the sneeze finally rose. She stifled it, not wanting to make any sound that would interrupt the Animals, who were on stage in the middle of singing "House of the Rising Sun." The crisis over, Meg went right back to swaying in time with the other dancers, looking over at Roxanne, who was sitting next to her. "You didn't say 'Bless you,'" Meg whispered.

Rox was staring off to the side of the stage, the place known as the wings. "Huh?" she said.

"I just sneezed," Meg told her impatiently, "and you didn't say 'Bless you.'"

"Bless you," Roxanne replied, still looking away from Meg.

Meg looked back at the Animals. They were most of the way through their song. Meg liked the band a lot, but she had seen them once before, and had heard "House of the Rising Sun" a million times already. Besides, she had more important things occupying her mind. "I have not been able to stop thinking about Drew," she told Rox. "I've tried and tried, but I can't focus on anything—not school, not music, nothing! I wasn't like this around Jimmy or Luke. Isn't that weird? Did you get like that when you first met Lenny?"

"Uh-huh," Roxanne answered, her eyes still glued to the wings.

Meg found herself annoyed that Rox wasn't listening. She leaned over to try and see what her friend was staring at. "What's so interesting over there, anyway?" she whispered.

Out of the main lights, in the shadows to the side of the stage, Meg could see Lenny. Meg didn't think he was that handsome, personally, but there were times, when the light was right, or when Lenny was wearing certain clothes, or when he smiled a particular way, that Meg thought she could see why Rox liked Lenny so much. There was something appealing about him. Plus he was nice, kind, and a pretty talented bass player, and he certainly seemed to like Roxanne. In fact, he treated her like a queen.

Right now, however, Lenny was talking to Sherry Mann.

"What are they talking about?" Rox asked Meg urgently.

Meg sighed, exasperated. She wanted advice about her feelings for Drew, and Rox gave the best advice of anyone she knew. Roxanne was a lot wilder than Meg, and a lot more experienced. But she understood Meg in a way that none of her friends ever had before, and certainly in ways her family never could.

But then Meg's exasperation cooled as she realized that, even without a conversation, Rox had given her advice. Just by seeing how worked up Roxanne was getting over Lenny, Meg knew she wasn't the only one whose thoughts could be totally dominated by a guy.

Meg looked again at Sherry, and shook her head. "She's probably just asking him advice about working at *Bandstand*," Meg said reassuringly. "You heard her—she's just trying to get to know people here."

Rox frowned. "Lenny sure looks like he's having a good time talking to her," she muttered. "Do you think she's pretty?"

"Not even," Meg replied instantly. She knew better than to answer the question honestly. The truth was the *last* thing Roxanne wanted to hear right now. "She doesn't hold a candle to you, and I'm sure that, even if she is trying to make a move on Lenny, he's telling her that he's completely in love with you. If he looks like he's being friendly to her, it's only because he's probably trying to be polite and let her down easy."

Roxanne didn't look convinced at all. She kept staring daggers at Lenny and the girl. "Maybe," she said.

The Animals ended "House of the Rising Sun" with a single held chord, and all the dancers rose from their seats in the bleachers to applaud enthusiastically. Even though Meg didn't feel particularly enthusiastic about the music today, she dutifully smiled and screamed as she clapped. It was all part of show business.

Dick Clark, the show's star and host, stepped behind the podium, thanked his musical guests, and said good-bye, saluting to the camera as he always did. The show's theme song, "Bandstand Boogie," kicked in, and the dancers crowded onto the stage floor to dance. Meg traded steps with Rox, but Roxanne looked every few seconds into the wings. Lenny and Sherry Mann stood side-by-side, watching the dancers and smiling.

The music faded away, and Colin walked out onto the floor, holding his clipboard. "Good show, everyone, a ripper," he complimented them in his

British accent. "Remember, the Kinks are coming back next Saturday, so keep that energy up." He applauded them as he walked away, and the dancers joined in. Then everyone started to drift apart in their own small groups, leaving the studio.

Roxanne started immediately for the wings, but Meg quickly caught up to her and gently took her friend's elbow. "Roxanne, wait," she said.

Rox turned around impatiently. "I don't want to wait," Rox told her. "I want to know what's going on with Lenny and that girl, and I want to know right now. Girls love musicians. No one knows that better than me! Lenny's going to have lots of girls chasing him, and I need to know if he's going to jump for every one he sees!"

"Okay, but you don't want to look upset or jealous," Meg pointed out, "or Lenny will think you're possessive."

"I definitely don't want that," Rox admitted.

"So play it cool," Meg went on. "You don't know what he was talking to her about, and it could have been anything. You don't want to be the girl who tells him he can't talk to anyone else. I wouldn't want a boy telling me that."

Roxanne nodded. "That's true."

"So be casual," Meg suggested. "See what you

can find out without seeming like you're trying to find out anything."

Rox looked at Meg seriously for a long moment, then broke into laughter. Meg felt herself becoming annoyed. "What's so funny?"

"It's just, usually I'm the one giving you romantic advice," Roxanne said, now laughing so hard she could barely catch her breath. "I'm not used to it being the other way around!"

Meg had to laugh too. It *was* pretty funny, actually. "I guess I just had a good teacher," she said through her giggles.

Now Roxanne took Meg's elbow. "Come on," she said, "let's go be casual."

Meg held back. "You want me to go with you?"

"Yeah," Rox answered. "That way it won't seem like I'm trying to corner Lenny or something."

The two girls moved from the center of the stage to the wings. Lenny was talking to Sherry again. Meg took a moment to really look at the girl a second time. She was even prettier up close than she was from a distance. If she really was interested in Lenny, Roxanne might be in a lot of trouble.

Lenny looked up as Meg and Roxanne approached. He got a nervous look on his face, and quickly said good-bye to the pretty girl. Puzzled, she walked away as Lenny moved forward to meet Meg and Roxanne. It was almost, Meg thought, like Lenny was trying to keep himself between Sherry and Roxanne.

"Hey," he said to them by way of greeting. "Great show today, wasn't it? Did you see Hilton Valentine? The Animals' guitarist? I heard he's left-handed, but he had to learn right-handed and so he does all the chords upside down!" He pantomimed the awkwardness of playing with his left hand, shaking his head incredulously. "Oh, and hey, I really liked how you two were dancing today. Good stuff."

Roxanne smiled, and Meg was impressed by how well Rox was keeping her cool. When Rox lost her temper, grizzly bears had been known to go running, and Communists had been known to surrender their rifles in fear. "You saw us dancing? It looked like you were pretty busy during the taping."

Lenny gave her a kiss on the cheek. "I always make sure I sneak a peek or two at my girl during the show," he assured her.

"That's so sweet," Roxanne said, turning to Meg. "Isn't it?"

Meg nodded vigorously. "Sweet," she agreed.

Then a long silence fell as the three of them smiled stiffly at each other, each waiting for someone else to say something. Meg was almost going to ask, "How about this weather?" or, "I think the Phillies will be pretty good next year, how about you?" just to have something to say.

But finally, Roxanne broke the silence, asking Lenny, "So, are you almost done with work? I'm starving, and I can't wait to try that new diner, like we talked about."

Lenny looked pained, and slapped a hand to his forehead. "Aw, Rox, I completely forgot we talked about doing that," he said. "I made some other plans, and I can't change 'em. I'll make it up to you, and we'll go another time."

Roxanne's smile stayed frozen on her face. "Other plans" was all she said, as though inviting Lenny to give a more complete explanation. To Meg, it felt like the studio had become ten degrees colder in the last thirty seconds.

Lenny nodded. "Yeah," he answered. "Band practice. With the band. I'm really sorry."

Meg looked over at her best friend, and could sense, rather than see, the anger building up beneath that smile. Here came the volcano, and Meg was about to have a ringside seat for the eruption. *Don't do it,* Meg thought, her voice so loud in her own head she hoped Roxanne might actually hear her.

Miraculously, Rox followed Meg's mental order. "Don't worry about it," she told her boyfriend. "I hope your band practice goes well."

Lenny leaned down and kissed Roxanne again. "I'll see you when I see you," he said, and walked away. Rox watched him go, her dark eyes focused on his back, her face drawn into a worried scowl.

"'Band practice,'" she repeated. "'With the band.' I'm glad he told me, because I was wondering who he would be having band practice with."

"He practices with the band all the time," Meg reminded Roxanne. "He could be telling the truth."

Roxanne chewed on her lower lip. "I don't know," she said. "There was something pretty different about how he was talking. It was like he was definitely hiding something he didn't want to tell me."

"Your mind is playing tricks on you," Meg said, trying to sound more confident than she was. "Lenny thinks you hung the moon." Meg wasn't sure what that phrase meant, but she'd heard her mother use it in describing how she felt when she'd first seen Meg's father. "I'm sure it's nothing."

"I hope you're right," Roxanne said, her voice barely a whisper.

Three

The gray sky had broken up a bit and now held a touch of late afternoon gold as Meg walked across the campus of the University of Pennsylvania. The trees had some yellow in their leaves, a few of which were already dotting the emerald grass between the dignified buildings and wide sidewalks. Everyone she passed seemed to be wearing a sweatshirt that said, PENN, or QUAKERS.

They all carried books or briefcases, looking like they had important places to be, and important things to study, even on the weekend. Some sat on benches, or even on the grass, reading alone, studying together, or discussing class topics or shooting the breeze in groups. The energy was contagious, and Meg loved catching it. The more time she spent here, the more she couldn't wait for college, to be one of these people, to live in the center of it. *The only time I feel like this,* she thought, *is when I'm dancing on* Bandstand.

Trying to be casual, she looked left and right as

she walked, hoping against hope to maybe catch a glimpse of Drew. She pictured him walking out of an academic building, or perhaps the student union, in deep debate with other students, changing their minds about a meaningful topic . . . and then he'd look up and see Meg, and his eyes would light up, and his smile would shine, and then—

Meg shook her head, struggling to push away the thought. *Don't get ahead of yourself!*

But she couldn't help thinking about him. Meg had never met anybody like Drew before. He was somebody who understood the world, and had opinions about it. But not like Meg's father, Jack, had opinions. Her father seemed to have been born with his opinions—about Communism, about presidents, about whom Meg should date—and those opinions were what they were. There was certainly no changing his mind. Meg loved her father, and she was certain of his love for her, but he could be very strict, a condition that had only become more pronounced when it came to Meg as she moved further into her teenage years. It seemed as though the more she wanted to try new things and stretch her wings, the more he tried to hold her back. She'd tried to talk about it with him, but never got very far. There was very little room for discussion with Jack Pryor.

With Drew, there was always discussion. He loved to talk about the city, the country, the world. He had his opinions, but he had reasons for them, and he loved sharing them with Meg. He had a way of speaking that made people want to hear more, made them want to keep the conversation going for as long as possible. Meg, for her part, was happy to listen, learn, and just to be around Drew. And not only because he was, as Roxanne might say, "easy on the eyes." Which he was, with his sandy brown hair and twinkling eyes, not to mention his dimples— Meg was a sucker for dimples. And there was the matter of Drew's muscles. He had been a star lacrosse player in high school, and he hadn't lost his impressive physique.

But looks weren't everything for Meg when it came to Drew. Through Drew, Meg was learning there was a lot more to life than the same bus rides and routines. He had taught her there were all sorts of people, cultures, issues, and all sorts of changes happening every minute, around every corner.

Meg walked up the steps in front of the dormitory both Beth and Drew lived in. Meg reached for the door's handle, only to have it open from inside. She pulled her hand back just as Drew stepped out with four other students, three boys and one girl. One of the boys, a muscular guy with heavy, dark eyebrows, walked close to Drew, his eyes blazing with purpose. "I still say we should do whatever it takes to defend those homes, and I mean whatever it takes," he said.

Drew looked his friend right in the eye. "And I say we're going to defend those homes, Cliff, but we're going to do it the way we agreed on as a group. Majority rules, remember?"

The whole group started down the stairs, in a hurry. None of them had even seen Meg behind the door. Hesitantly, she stepped forward and called out, "Drew? Drew!"

At the bottom of the steps, the students stopped and turned around. Seeing her, Drew looked surprised and happy, but maybe not as happy as Meg hoped he might. "Meg," he said, dashing back up the steps. "What are you doing here, High School?"

High School was Drew's nickname for Meg, which was funny considering he wasn't that far removed from high school himself. Meg didn't really care for it, but she liked that Drew had a special name just for her.

Meg tried her best to sound nonchalant, but everything still came out in a babbling rush. "Oh, I just came by to see Beth. She's helping. With a family project. A care package. For my brother." Meg winced. *Really smooth,* she thought.

Cliff, the guy with the dark eyebrows, cleared his throat impatiently at the bottom of the steps. Drew looked back at him over his shoulder, then turned to face Meg, an apologetic look on his face. "I'm sorry, but we were just heading out."

Meg started back toward the door, deeply disappointed on the inside, but smiling on the outside. "That's okay," she said. "I'll just see you the next time I come by."

Drew put a hand on the door, keeping it closed before she could even move to open it. "Unless . . . ," he said, looking into her eyes. "Would you maybe want to come with us?"

"Sure," Meg replied, faster than she intended to.

Drew smiled. "Great," he said.

Cliff (Meg had already decided she was always going to think of him as the Eyebrow Guy) cleared his throat again, more insistently. Drew rolled his eyes so only Meg could see, and she stifled a laugh. They headed down the steps together and started off across campus at a brisk walk. "Guys, this is Meg

Pryor," Drew said. "She's a friend of Beth Mason's."

A friend of Beth Mason's? That wasn't exactly how Meg wanted to be introduced. *Girlfriend,* or even *the girl I'm seeing* . . . heck, even *the girl I'm* kind of *seeing* would have been closer to what Meg had in mind.

"Meg," he went on, "this is Dan, Greg, and Natalie."

"Hi," Meg said shyly to all of them. All three either said hello or nodded in return.

Drew then gestured to Eyebrow Guy. "And this is Cliff."

Cliff didn't even look at her. "Drew, we don't need extra baggage along," he said. "It's probably past her bedtime."

Meg blushed. But before she could say anything, Drew leaped to her defense. "Meg happens to be as committed to learning about social justice as anyone I know, Cliff. And if she wants to learn about what's going on around her, it's our duty to help her do that."

That shut Cliff up but good, his eyebrows knitting together like two strips of fabric, and he walked ahead of everyone else, scowling. Very quietly, so Cliff wouldn't hear, Meg leaned in toward Drew. "Where are we going, anyway?"

"We're going to the neighborhood just north of campus," Drew told her.

Meg's stomach fluttered a little. She'd seen the neighborhood on the news many times, generally in connection with some kind of crime. "That's not a very good neighborhood, is it?"

"It's a poor neighborhood," he corrected her. "That doesn't mean it isn't good. And the university is thinking about buying it so they can put up a new science center."

"A new science center? That sounds like a great idea," Meg said.

Drew shook his head sternly. "It's a terrible idea. There's nothing good about a new science center."

Meg was confused. "Why not?"

"A new science center means some university scientists—and university graduate students—will be working on projects for the government, and some of those could be for the military," Drew explained.

Cliff, who had drifted back to them, said over his shoulder, "Like Project Spice Rack."

"That sounds like something my mother would want in her kitchen," Meg joked. But no one laughed.

"Project Spice Rack has to do with chemical

weapons, Meg," Dan said patiently but seriously. "It's not about making bombs that kill people, but gases and diseases that kill people."

Thoughts suddenly raced in Meg's head about poisonous gases she might inhale without knowing it, falling victim to attackers she couldn't see. Surely no one would ever do something like release a deadly virus on unsuspecting people with no warning, would they? And surely *American soldiers* wouldn't be the ones doing it . . . would they? Meg couldn't ever picture JJ killing people with chemical weapons. In fact, she couldn't picture JJ killing anyone at all, but she supposed he might have to, if he went to war. But then, an even scarier image slithered into her brain: some enemy using weapons like the ones Drew was talking about to kill American soldiers like JJ. Chilled, Meg willed the image away.

"That's *if* Project Spice Rack is real," Drew pointed out. "It's just a rumor, as far as we know."

Cliff snorted at this, but Drew ignored him. "The really important thing," Drew went on, "is that if the university buys up this neighborhood to build the science center, it'll mean the residents will be forced out of their homes."

"And since most of the people who live in the

neighborhood are colored," Natalie continued, "that means it's practically enforced segregation—white people telling colored people where they can or can't live. And that's wrong."

Meg wasn't sure she understood all of what she was hearing. "The university can't *make* the people who live in the neighborhood move, can they?"

"No," Drew admitted. "But here's what they'll do: The university will buy all the businesses in the area. With no grocery stores, cleaners, restaurants, or hardware stores to support them, the people who live in the houses will take whatever the university will give them for their property, and it'll be less than what they're worth, that's for sure."

"Everyone will move out, and into even poorer neighborhoods, because that's all they'll be able to afford," Greg finished.

"That's awful," Meg said. She couldn't imagine being basically forced out of her own house.

"Assessors hired by the university are walking through the neighborhood right now, looking at the properties and figuring out how much they're supposedly worth," Drew told Meg. "We're heading over there to watch them work."

"We're just going to watch," Meg said, confused.

Cliff turned around and smiled. Meg thought he

looked almost sinister, like a comic-book villain looking forward to a particularly nasty plan. "Well, we might do a little more than watch," he said.

Drew smiled as well. "We've finally found the issue that could put the student voice on the map at this school and in this community."

Hearing the excitement in Drew's voice, Meg found it impossible to not be excited herself. Walking in the middle of this group, on such an important mission, she felt part of something, and it gave her a thrill that traveled from her toes all the way up the back of her neck.

As they walked, she watched the neighborhood transform around them, going from the well-manicured lawns and buildings of the college campus to cracked sidewalks and crumbling lots. An older black lady walked past them, wearing a moth-eaten coat and pulling a small metal laundry cart loaded with a few tins of cheap condensed milk and inexpensive canned vegetables, never even looking up at those who crossed her path on the street. In an empty lot filled with rubble and garbage, a group of young boys played stickball, using a broom handle to knock their raggedy ball off the brick facades of the buildings around them. Passing a run-down house, she saw a mother and her young son working in a threadbare garden, trying to make the sickly-looking plants look as nice as possible in the cold weather.

Meg paused a moment to watch the mother and son dig up soil, move dirt around, and pack it tightly around the base of the flowers and herbs. Meg had seen poverty before, and she'd traveled through some of the poorest neighborhoods in Philadelphia. But she'd never spent much real time in any of them, and she had never looked at them quite like this. For the first time, she started to see this neighborhood as somebody's home, as part of a community. People lived here, and while some undoubtedly wished they lived somewhere else, others wanted to make it a better place to live, a place to be proud of, a place that could prosper. And Meg found herself wanting to help them.

"There they are," Cliff growled, pointing up ahead. Meg followed his gesture, and saw two white men, with black-rimmed glasses, hats, tan over-coats, and shiny black shoes, crossing the street to a row of ramshackle homes. They carried clipboards and briefcases.

Cliff trotted up ahead, the others hurrying to keep up. "Cliff, slow down! Take it easy," Drew implored. Meg felt her heart start to race, thrilled to be part of a team going into action. She struggled to match Drew's pace, but he was an athlete, and moved with practiced grace and ease.

Cliff stepped in front of the assessors, blocking their path up the sidewalk to the nearest house. "How's it going, fellas?" he asked mischievously.

"Good afternoon, son," replied the older of the two men as Drew, Meg, and the others filled in behind Cliff. The younger assessor remained behind his superior, looking a little nervous.

"I'm sorry," Cliff replied. "But I'm not your son. And you're definitely not my dad."

The older man, who was nearly Cliff's size, only looked at them impatiently. "If you'll excuse us . . ." He tried to step past Cliff.

Cliff blocked his path, and Meg felt the others move to the side with him in what felt like a planned formation. Meg, going along, stepped to the side with them. *It's like doing the Locomotion,* she thought giddily. And just like that famous dance, it was best when done by a lot of people. Meg stole a glance up and to the side, at Drew standing next to her. His chin was set firmly, determination etched on his face. Meg felt part of something important and, even better, she was doing it with Drew.

"No problem," Cliff said, continuing to block the

assessors' path. "It's a nice day for a walk, isn't it?"

The older man squinted through his glasses at Cliff. "We don't want any trouble, son."

"Get your hearing checked, pal," Cliff snarled, puffing out his chest. "I'm still not your son!"

Drew quickly stepped up beside Cliff. "Sir, my name is Drew Mandel. We represent the concerned students of the University of Pennsylvania, and we're here in protest of what you're trying to do."

The younger of the two men peeked around his boss. "What we're trying to do, is our jobs," he said meekly.

"And you don't care who gets thrown out of their houses when you do it," Cliff retorted, jabbing a finger in his face.

Drew put a hand on Cliff's shoulder. "Just calm down, Cliff," he said. But Meg didn't think Cliff was interested in calming down. The air suddenly felt a little colder, the sky seemed a little darker, and Meg didn't have such a good feeling anymore. She could feel Dan, Greg, and Natalie standing tensely beside her.

"If you have a problem with what we're doing," the older man said with a hint of very controlled anger behind his polite words, "I suggest you take it up with your university's Board of Trustees."

"We're doing just that," Drew said calmly, standing up straight. Meg thought he looked so proud and strong. "We're making sure they know we're standing up for the people who live here. In the meantime, the school doesn't own this sidewalk, and we're allowed to stand wherever we like on it."

The assessors looked at him, as though considering their next move. Glancing up, Meg could see a few black faces leaning out their windows, some concerned, others worried. In the street around them, a few of the neighborhood's residents had come out to see what was going on, standing quietly nearby.

Finally, the assessors stepped off the sidewalk and into the street, intending to walk around the students that way. But Cliff jumped off the curb and stood in front of them, the others following just behind to take up positions over his shoulder. "Of course, we could stand in the street, too," Cliff said, smiling. "That's public property, just like the sidewalk."

The older assessor sighed, out of patience, and tried to push past Cliff, putting a meaty hand on Cliff's muscular bicep. "You kids have made your point," he said gruffly. "But there's nothing we can do about it, so—"

Cliff roughly yanked the assessor's hand off his arm. "Don't touch me, man," he shouted. He shoved the older man in the chest, making him stumble back several steps. His briefcase went flying, papers spilling out everywhere. The man recovered, balling his hands into fists, and taking a menacing step at Cliff. Cliff tensed, ready to fight, a willing smile on his face. The younger assessor looked around, frightened, as though he felt trapped. Meg knew the feeling. The world seemed to be spinning out of control, and her mind raced back to the previous summer, to the craziness and chaos of the riots. It felt like it was all about to happen again, and this time she wasn't just in the center of it, she was among the people who might be starting it. She wanted to be away from here. She wanted to be home. But she wanted to stay with Drew, too.

Drew hastily stepped around Cliff, getting between the two men. "Cliff, stop it! We didn't come here to fight!"

Cliff pushed Drew now, keeping his eyes fixed on the assessor. "Sure we did, Drew! We came here to fight for these houses and the people who live here," he argued.

"And that's what we're doing," he reminded Cliff. "But we're not going to do it with violence! If we throw punches, our issues will never be taken seriously, and we'll never have a voice in how things get done!"

Meg couldn't have been prouder of Drew than she was at that moment. He was absolutely right. She wanted no part of a fight, and from her quick looks at the faces of Natalie, Greg, and Dan, Meg didn't think they wanted to fight, either. But Cliff didn't seem so sure. He tried to push through Drew to get to the older man, and Drew was just barely able to hold him back.

It's about to happen again, Meg thought with dread.

But suddenly a police car screeched onto the street, its siren blaring. They all turned to the sound, Cliff stepping away from Drew, the older assessor backing up as well, letting his fists relax. After the car parked, two officers stepped from the car and pulled their nightsticks. "Does someone want to explain what's going on here?"

The officer that asked the question had sandy hair flecked with gray under his cap, and a pot belly. The other officer was skinny, with worried, droopy eyes, and nervous fingers that fiddled at his heavy belt. He looked familiar to Meg, but she couldn't place where she might have seen him before.

Drew and the older assessor stepped forward. "This is a nonviolent student protest," Drew explained.

"Uh-huh," the heavier cop replied. "It looked like it was about to become the most nonviolent street fight in history."

The older assessor, still angry, tried to plead his case. "We have a job to do, officer, and these punks are keeping us from doing it!"

The policeman shook his head. "Right now, all of you are just disturbing the peace, so I'm going to ask you to disperse. Go back home, or to your dorms, or to your offices, or wherever."

"But . . . ," the assessor and Cliff said at the same time.

Drew silenced Cliff with a stern look. The officer said the rest. "No buts. I want all of you off this street, right now."

The assessor muttered under his breath, and started gathering up his scattered papers. Cliff turned around and stalked off, followed by Dan, Greg, and Natalie. The skinny officer walked up to Meg uncertainly. "Do you need a ride home, miss?"

Meg looked from the officer to Drew, and back. "No," she said, quickly, pointing to Drew. "I'm with him."

The officer looked strangely at both of them, then seemed to understand. "Okay. I guess. Be safe, now." As the assessors walked the other direction, the officers got back in their car and drove away. Meg couldn't shake the feeling that she knew the officer from somewhere, and this seemed to back that up—why else would he single her out to talk to? But she still couldn't place him.

Drew put an arm around her shoulder, and his simple touch made all her other thoughts and worries go away. "Come on, High School," he said quietly, "let's get back to campus."

Meg and Drew walked mostly in silence as the blight of the poor neighborhood gave way to the nicer buildings of the school. Meg wasn't sure what to say. On the one hand, she loved being with Drew at the center of action that was meant to make a difference in the community. But on the other, she wasn't so sure she wanted to be a protestor if all the protests were going to turn out to be so crazy and almost violent.

Finally, Drew spoke, having almost seemed to read her mind. "I'm sorry about what happened back there," he said to her as they walked through the halls of his dorm. "It wasn't supposed to get ugly like that."

"I wasn't scared," she lied.

"Cliff's kind of a loose cannon," Drew went on with a frown. "That's not how we're going to change things in this country."

Meg nodded. "Yeah."

He stopped in the hallway, leaned back against a wall, and smiled warmly at her. "You really stood up in the face of what was going on," he said quietly. "I'm glad you were there with me,"

Meg looked down at her shoes, smiling with happy embarrassment. "Me too," she replied.

"We're going back out a week from tomorrow, next Sunday, to protest more assessments," he said. "The assessors like to go around on weekends, when people are out of town or in church, so there's no one to hassle them. I'd love for you to come along, if you still want to be part of things."

Meg wanted nothing more in the whole world than to continue to be part of whatever Drew was doing. "I'd love to," she answered. "You can count on me."

Drew stepped close to her. "That's what I like to hear," he said, and gave her a soft kiss.

When they broke away from each other, Meg looked into his eyes. She could have stayed there forever. But . . .

"I'd better go find Beth," she said reluctantly. "We have to work on that care package."

"In that case, I'll see you later," Drew replied.

Meg gave him a little wave as she moved down the hall away from him. He waved back. Meg continued on to Beth's room, all thoughts of the tense street confrontation driven away by Drew's kiss.

Four

Beth sealed an envelope around a letter to JJ she had just completed, then held up a small bottle of perfume to show Meg, who sat on the edge of Beth's bed, watching intently. "And now, for the final touch," she said, then squirted just a touch of perfume on both the front and the back of the envelope. "Never underestimate the sense of smell when dealing with men, Meg," Beth continued.

She put down the perfumed envelope and turned to a stack of similar envelopes—letters Beth had written in the few days before. The Righteous Brothers crooned "You've Lost That Lovin' Feeling" through Beth's radio. "Do you write JJ every day?" Meg asked.

"I try," Beth told her. "A lot of times, I feel bad, though, like I'm writing the same things over and over. 'I miss you. I miss you. I miss you.' It's probably boring him to death."

Meg smiled. "I bet he doesn't care. I bet you could copy a page from the dictionary, and JJ wouldn't mind, because it was from you."

Beth smiled in return, and kept working her way through the letters. "Sometimes it's hard to study," Beth admitted. "Or even to listen in class. My mind will just go somewhere else when I'm reading a textbook or listening to a professor. I'll have whole conversations in my head with JJ, and they'll seem so real that I'll actually hear his voice. Or I'll think about how many miles away he is and count the states between us, then think of the capitals of those states . . ." She looked up, slightly embarrassed. "Do you think that means I'm crazy?"

"I think that means you're in love," Meg replied seriously.

Beth laughed. "I'm definitely that. Speaking of which, how are things with you and Mr. Mandel down the hall?"

Meg sat up a little straighter, surprised. "Drew? And me? Oh, we're not in love! No, we're just friends. Love? No, no, no, no, no."

"Meg," Beth asked gently, smiling. "Have you ever heard the quote, 'The lady doth protest too much, methinks'?"

"No."

"It means you're saying *no* so many times, I'm starting to believe you really mean *yes.*"

Meg thought about arguing for a moment, then said, "I don't know if Drew's in love. You'd have to ask him."

Beth smiled again, sympathetically. "Drew's a great guy."

"It's just . . . ," Meg started.

Beth pushed the letters aside and leaned forward on her desk, looking at Meg, concerned. "What is it?"

Meg smoothed out her skirt, more to give her hands something to do than because her skirt needed smoothing. "It's just, I know how I feel about him, and sometimes I think I know how he feels about me, but then, in a second, it seems like everything changes and I don't have any idea again."

Beth nodded in understanding. "Drew's got a lot going on. Not just classes, but all of his activism stuff, and athletics, too."

"I know, I know," Meg said. "I'd just like to be somewhere in there, too."

"I'm sure you are," Beth said, getting up from her desk and moving over to sit with Meg on the bed. "Listen, it's early. You practically just met. Give it time and let it grow a little. There's no reason to rush."

Meg nodded. Beth was right, but that didn't

mean Meg had an easy job ahead of her. Slowing down the heart was not a simple task.

The door opened, and Marlene, Beth's freckle-faced neighbor in the dorm, poked her head in. "Beth, you've got a phone call. It's JJ."

Meg and Beth traded excited looks. "Do you want to say hi?" Beth asked.

Meg didn't even have to answer. The two girls raced out into the hallway, and Beth scooped up the receiver dangling from the pay phone. "JJ?" she practically shouted. "Hi! Oh, I miss you, too! Listen, there's someone here who wants to say hello. I know, I know, you don't have much time. I'll get right back on. Here you go." She handed the receiver to Meg.

"Hi, JJ," Meg said, almost shyly.

"Meg, is that you?" JJ's voice crackled down the line to her. He sounded like he was calling from another planet. "How are you?"

"I'm the same, I'm fine! JJ, how are *you*?"

"I'm bored. I'm doing drills in my sleep, it feels like. How's Thrill? Is he doing okay?"

"Basically," Meg told him. Their little brother Will idolized JJ; he was everything Will wanted to be. And Will was as nice, as kind, and as devoted to his family as his older brother was. Unfortunately, Will hadn't been able to follow in JJ's impressive footsteps in sports like football. Because of polio, Will walked with a heavy brace on his leg. Meg knew their parents were thinking about an experimental operation for Will that might allow him to walk normally. Meg's mother didn't want Will to know too many details; she didn't want him to get his hopes up. Unfortunately, Will knew just enough to be scared, and no one would tell him any more.

Meg decided to change the subject. "JJ, do you have any idea if you'll be going anywhere?"

There was a long pause on the other end of the line. "No one's sure. There's been some talk about maybe Okinawa sometime soon, but . . ."

Meg's heart skipped a beat. Viet Nam was bad enough, but . . . "Where's Okinawa?"

"Just off of Japan," JJ told her. "Listen, Meg, I'm going to call home in the next couple days, if I can, so . . ."

"I understand," Meg said in a rush. "Here, I'll put Beth back on and talk to you later."

Meg was just about to pass the phone to Beth when she heard JJ's tinny voice come through the earpiece. "Wait! Meg, are you still there?"

She quickly pressed the phone back to her ear. "I'm here, JJ! What's the matter?"

"Nothing, just . . . I miss you guys. I miss you."

Meg felt tears rising to her eyes, and a lump swelling in her throat. "We miss you too, JJ."

There was a long pause on her brother's end of the line. JJ didn't often let his emotions get the better of him, so it was hard for Meg to imagine what was going on at Camp Lejeune, but she thought she could guess. "All right, be good," JJ said finally.

"You too." Meg handed over the phone to Beth, a little sad to do so. Hearing JJ's voice was comforting, settling down her roller-coaster feelings about Drew.

"Hi, JJ," Beth said, leaning dreamily against the wall. Meg stood still for a moment, then realized that she wasn't needed here anymore. She waved to get Beth's attention and, when she did, gestured back over her shoulder to Beth's room, indicating that she'd pick up the letters and the perfume bottle for JJ's care package and depart. Beth nodded and waved back, smiling.

Meg started down the hall, pausing only once to look back over her shoulder. She saw the look on Beth's face, and wished for a feeling like that to call her own. *Give it time,* she thought, remembering Beth's advice.

Five

"**W**hat about you, Pete?" Meg's father, Jack, asked his younger brother across the Pryor family dinner table. "You want to put anything into JJ's care package?"

Uncle Pete, who was still wearing his policeman's uniform, took a steaming dish of carrots from Will as he thought over his answer. "I don't know. I'm not really sure I have anything— Thanks, Thrill."

"Welcome," Will replied around a mouthful of roast beef.

"Mouth closed, Will, please," Meg's mom, Helen, reminded the youngest of the Pryors' four children before turning to Pete as she spooned rice onto her plate. "It would mean so much to JJ if there was something in there from you, Pete. Anything to remind him of home."

Uncle Pete snapped his fingers. "Got it," he said. "I could send him a bunch of sports pages from the *Inquirer*, get him caught up on basketball! Between those kids Hal Greer and Chet Walker, this should be the year our Sixers finally take down those Celtics!"

"JJ would love that," Will said, more food spilling from his mouth.

"What did your mother just say, Thrill," his father admonished, then raised a glass to Pete. "Good thing you never throw out your newspapers, little brother."

"If we keep cutting down trees to make paper and furniture and other things, the world will be completely out of trees by 1979," Patty chimed in. She looked up from her dinner to see everyone staring at her, and shrugged. "That's what I read, at least."

Jack nodded, not really sure what to say, which was often the case for the Pryor family when it came to Patty. He turned to Meg. "What did Beth put in?"

Meg poked at her food. "Some perfume, and a bunch of letters."

"JJ wears perfume?" Will asked, surprised, his fork stopped halfway to his mouth.

Helen smiled warmly. "I think it's to remind JJ of a smell he likes, Will."

Will finished taking his bite. "Oh," he said, relieved.

"JJ called while I was over at Beth's," Meg added.

Everyone stopped eating simultaneously, and all eyes focused on Meg. "JJ called? Is he all right?" her mother asked worriedly.

"I think he's fine. He was just calling to talk to Beth. To say hi, I guess."

"Did you talk to him?" Patty wanted to know.

"Did he ask about me?" Will wondered, his words overlapping Patty's.

"I talked to him. He asked about you," Meg assured Will, then turned to her family. "He asked about everyone. He's going to try and call in the next few days."

Her father leaned back in his chair, his voice quiet. "Did he say anything about when they'd be shipping out?"

"No," Meg told him. "He said some of the marines were talking about Okinawa."

Jack looked across the table at his wife. Helen's eyes filled with tears, and Meg could read her father's unspoken admonition to her mother: *Don't cry, not in front of the kids. JJ will be fine. Be strong.* Everyone sat silently, their thoughts on their absent brother, son, and nephew.

At last, Jack dropped his fork to his plate, the clatter signaling a change in subject and a request for attention. "Okay, everyone, I've given it a lot of thought . . ."

Meg, Patty, and Will all looked at their father with alarm. Usually, when he started out like this, it meant an increase in their household chores.

"It's time for the return of the Pryor Family Movie Outing," he announced.

"Really?" Will asked, his eyes lighting up with excitement. "Can we see *Santa Claus Conquers the Martians*?"

"No!" Patty cut him off. "I don't want to see that. We should see *Dr. Strangelove*!"

"*Dr. Strangelove*?" Will asked, puzzled. "He sounds like he's from outer space! Is he?"

"I've heard the new James Bond movie is pretty good," Pete contributed. "What's it called—*Goldfinger.*"

Helen smiled at Jack, surprised. "A movie, Jack?"

Jack nodded. "It's been too long since we've done something like that as a family, and with JJ away, it's more important than ever that we stick together."

"I think it's a great idea. When were you thinking about?" Helen wanted to know.

"Next Sunday afternoon," Jack replied.

Meg felt her heart skip a beat. Sunday was when she was supposed to join Drew to protest the science center! There was no way she could risk losing the chance to be with Drew to spend time with her family at a movie she probably wasn't going to want to see anyway. "Um," she said, tentatively, "I think I'm already busy that afternoon."

The table fell silent again, and once more all eyes turned to Meg. She could hear the disappointment and mild anger in her father's voice. "Yeah? What do you have going on?"

"Just stuff," Meg answered evasively. She knew her father would never approve of what she had planned. But she also knew he wouldn't be satisfied with so vague an answer.

"Define *stuff*," Jack asked, an edge rising in his request.

Jack had barely let Meg out of his sight since the riots, demanding to know where she was, who she was with, and what she was doing every second of every day. It had been a struggle to even get him to agree to let her take the bus to Vinyl Crocodile, to WFIL, or to Penn to visit Beth—and, secretly, Drew. It was a wonder, Meg thought, that her father hadn't started building a bomb shelter under their backyard so he could keep his kids there all the time.

Though Meg could understand her father's protective attitude, it bothered her anyway. She was more than able to take care of herself and recognize a bad situation before walking into it. The riots had been a random thing that couldn't be predicted. Meg couldn't be blamed for it, yet her father seemed to think otherwise.

The best defense is a good offense. That was something JJ had told Meg his football coach often said, meaning that if you wanted to win, you had to keep your opponent off balance. And Meg didn't want to tell her dad her real plans. So she decided to turn the tables. "Dad, I'm sixteen years old," Meg snapped back. "That's old enough to make my own plans, and you can't expect me to change them just because you've got something else in mind!"

Jack looked at Helen incredulously, as if to say, *Can you believe this?* Will and Patty looked at each other the same way, although with a little more excitement in their eyes. Watching their older sister challenge their father was very informative—it helped them know what they could and couldn't get away with when they got to be Meg's age.

Jack looked back to Meg, smiling calmly, though his face was turning bright red with anger. If the kids needed more proof of how angry he was, they could hear it in the quiet of his voice. When Jack Pryor was mad, he yelled. When he was *really* mad, his voice barely rose above a whisper. "Well, Miss I'm-Sixteen, you still live under my roof, and that means I get to know what you're going to be doing."

Meg knew he meant it. And she knew the smart play was to back down. But this was an important matter to her. And the highest of stakes were involved—a chance to spend time with Drew!

Meg knew it was the moment of truth. But the question was, how much truth could she tell? "If you must know," Meg huffed, "I'm going to be at Penn . . . visiting Beth . . . and her friends."

Jack nodded, an implied request for more information. "And what will you and Beth and Beth's friends—"

"Meg, your father will think about it," Helen suddenly cut in.

Jack's eyes shot to Helen with an angry glare. Helen looked right back at him, holding firm. Meg could tell that a discussion was going to be taking place between her parents sometime soon. But that didn't concern her. All Meg cared about was that she had a chance. She smiled a small smile down into her plate, one her father couldn't see, and went on eating her dinner.

• • •

Meg's smile returned later, after the meal, as she cleared the family's plates into the kitchen. She even caught herself quietly singing the song she had made up earlier in the Vinyl Crocodile. "Even though right now I'm here with you, in my heart I'm waving good-bye . . ."

Turning from the sink, she was startled to see Uncle Pete standing in the doorway to the dining room, holding his plate, and smiling crookedly at her. Meg felt herself blush and grin in return. "No, no," Pete said. "Sounds great to me. Is that the latest and greatest tune, the best of the tracks from the stacks of wax?"

Meg rolled her eyes and giggled. "Uncle Pete." Uncle Pete always could make her laugh. He had been through lots of rough times, bouncing from girlfriend to girlfriend, and Meg suspected that her parents worried Pete might like to drink a little too much alcohol. But he was always in a good mood around Meg, always had a joke or a wink for her that made them both smile. Maybe, Meg reflected, it was because both of them fought with her father so much. Each could understand what the other was going through.

Uncle Pete set his plate down on the kitchen table and took three oranges from the bowl in the table's center. "Think fast!" he said, tossing her the oranges one after the other.

Meg gave a little yelp. She managed to catch the first orange, barely, but the second bounced off her hand. The third she missed entirely, and it rolled across the kitchen floor. She and Pete dissolved into laughter, scooping the oranges up and putting them back into the bowl. "Don't tell your mother," Pete advised between bursts of laughter. "Come to think of it, don't tell your *father*!"

"Don't worry," Meg assured him, looking over her shoulder at the entrance to the dining room to make sure they hadn't been heard. "I won't tell them anything!"

"Uh-huh," Pete said, standing up and looking at Meg strangely. "Say, Meg, you've been spending a lot of time over at Penn with Beth, right? She sure is terrific. Your brother has great taste."

"Beth's almost like another sister to me," Meg told him. "I like spending time with her."

"Uh-huh," Pete said again. "And Penn's a pretty neat place, too, isn't it?"

"It's great," Meg agreed, a little confused. This was a strange conversation for them to be having.

"Meg," Pete went on, "do you remember Buddy Kelley?"

•

The name sounded sort of familiar to Meg, but she couldn't place it. "Not really," she admitted.

"He was in the police academy with me? Long, tall drink of water with droopy eyes, looks kind of like Huckleberry Hound?"

Meg felt butterflies start to whirl in her stomach . . . and not the good kind she felt when she was around Drew. She kept silent and looked away from her uncle, who sat down in a chair at the kitchen table.

"Anyways," Pete continued, "Buddy told me he and his partner Floyd Guthrie got called to some kind of near dust-up today, between these kids from Penn and a couple of business guys in bad suits. And here's the weird thing: He told me he saw a girl there who looked just like you. But he hadn't seen you in so long, he wasn't sure."

Meg still wouldn't look up at him. She couldn't lie to him, either. "It was me," she said.

Pete nodded slowly. He didn't look particularly upset, maybe a little worried. "So, your plans for Sunday," he went on. "Would they have anything to do with the people you were with this afternoon?"

Meg let the question hang in the warm air of the kitchen for a long moment, scuffing her feet over the tile floor. She really, really didn't want to answer.

The best defense is a good offense. Instead of answering, she presented her uncle Pete with a question of her own. "Are you going to tell my dad?" she asked quietly.

Uncle Pete picked up an apple from the bowl of fruit on the table and turned it over and over in his hand, as though checking it for the answer he was looking for, or maybe just some signs that worms had invaded. "You know your dad wouldn't want you out there, in a neighborhood like that, getting in trouble."

Meg nodded, but said nothing.

"But at the same time," Uncle Pete continued, " I know what you're saying about being sixteen and wanting to have your own life." He chuckled. "Lord knows, when I was sixteen, I went my own way enough times. Just ask your dad. Usually, he was the one who had to go out and bring me back."

Meg smiled at him hopefully. Uncle Pete smiled in return.

"I won't tell your dad this time," he said. "But I can't make any promises for next time. You just be careful, Meg. I don't want anything happening to my tied-for-first favorite niece."

Meg heaved a huge sigh of relief. But before she could even thank her uncle, Patty and Helen walked into the kitchen with more dishes. "And speaking of nieces," Pete said, putting his arm around Patty's shoulders and pulling her close, "here's the other young lady sharing first place on my list!"

Patty frowned, pulling away from him. "If you want to pick a favorite niece from between Meg and I . . . ," she started.

"'Meg and *me*,'" Helen corrected.

". . . we could have a spelling contest, or something," Patty finished.

Uncle Pete tossed the apple up in the air and caught it. "Nah, I'd rather keep it a tie," he said, winking privately at Meg. "It keeps you girls honest." He bit into the apple and walked back into the dining room.

Meg's mother laid the dishes in the sink and smiled at Meg. "What were the two of you talking about in here?"

Meg busied herself stacking dishes neatly on top of each other. "Nothing," she assured her mother.

As Helen turned on the hot water, Meg again sighed with relief, this time on the inside. She had made a narrow escape. If her dad had found out about the trouble she had nearly gotten into with Drew, there would have been no way he would have let Meg spend Sunday afternoon at Penn—or any other day.

Meg looked up at her mother, who was washing the dishes without a clue in the world as to Meg's inner thoughts. Meg was surprised to find she felt a little guilty. But she said nothing.

Six

"**I** used to tell my family everything," Meg moaned, drumming her fingertips against the counter at Vinyl Crocodile on Monday after school. The Supremes' new single was playing on the shop's hi-fi, and to Meg's great disappointment, "I'm Waving Good-bye" didn't sound anything like the song she'd made up. Luke had been right—the song wasn't very good.

But Meg wasn't all that concerned about the song at this particular moment. She couldn't get her conversation with Uncle Pete from the night before out of her mind. When had she become the kind of girl who kept secrets from her parents? Meg could remember heart-to-heart talks with her parents, both of them, in which she'd tell them exactly how she was feeling, exactly what she was doing. And they'd be happy to listen, and they'd give great advice, and Meg would always feel better afterward.

Now Meg felt like a thief, or a criminal of some kind. She felt like she had a pile of secrets hidden under her bed, or in the back of one of her drawers, buried in the dark where they couldn't be seen. She wasn't lying to her parents, but she wasn't telling them the whole truth, either. Meg just knew they wouldn't understand, or let her do these things that were so important to her. Meg knew that she was doing the right thing keeping some parts of her life secret from her parents. But that didn't make her feel good about it.

What Meg really needed was advice on how to deal with these feelings. She needed advice from her best friend. But Roxanne was in a world of her own, drumming her own fingers on the counter in an annoyingly different rhythm from Meg's, constantly checking her watch, constantly looking out the front door of Vinyl Crocodile. She was so distracted she had already ignored three customers who had been standing right in front of her, forcing Luke, who seemed extra grumpy today, to stomp over from where he was stocking the new releases.

"Come on, Roxanne," Luke would growl, "snap out of it!" Then he'd stomp back to the record bins.

"I'm a terrible daughter," Meg said to Roxanne. "I'm a terrible *person*. I'd tell Father Ryan, if I didn't know he'd run right to my parents."

Roxanne looked out the front door for the thirty-seventh time. "Father Ryan *can't* tell your parents. Whatever you say to him stays between the two of you. Well, and God, I suppose. That's the one great thing about confession."

"I think that only works if you're an adult," Meg said miserably. "I remember once, when I was seven, I confessed to stealing three Tootsie Rolls. Father Hanratty walked right out of the confessional and told my parents on the spot."

This made Roxanne turn. "*You* stole Tootsie Rolls?"

"Just that one time, but that's not the point!"

Roxanne sighed impatiently, checking her watch again. "Look, you haven't done anything wrong," she told Meg. "Your uncle's sticking up for you about what happened yesterday."

"Okay, fine," Meg replied. "But what about Sunday? What about the next time I'm supposed to see Drew?"

Roxanne moved from behind the counter to look out the front door, as if from where she stood at the register, she couldn't see the exact same thing. At the same time, a customer approached with a stack of 45s. "Big deal," she said to Meg. "You said you were going to be with Beth's friends, and that's exactly what Drew is—Beth's friend!"

"But what about not being with my family on Sunday," Meg groaned. "You didn't see my dad's face—he looked so excited when he brought up the idea of getting together for a movie! It's really important to him. What about that?"

"Excuse me," the customer tried to interject, holding up his 45s for someone to see. He was short, pimply, and shy-looking, probably two years older than Meg and Roxanne.

"But, nothing!" Roxanne exclaimed, whirling from the door to face Meg. It was almost as though she were angry with Meg for not understanding something that, to Roxanne, seemed so simple. "You're a teenager, Meg! It's practically your *responsibility* to ditch your family to be with Drew!"

Luke stomped over from the record bins, glaring at Roxanne as he moved behind the register. "Come on, Roxanne, will you snap out of it, *please*?" He angrily pushed buttons on the register, ringing up the sale. "This is *not* how you treat customers!"

The grateful customer smiled at Luke. "Thanks very much," he said, then pointed to the hi-fi speaker, indicating the Supremes' song, which was still playing. "Great new song, huh?"

Luke didn't look up, stabbing buttons. "Yeah, if you like garbage."

Roxanne elbowed Meg, muttering, "*That's* how you treat customers, I guess."

The customer didn't say anything else as Luke shoved all the 45s into a bag. Instead, he just got out of the store as quickly as he could, not looking at any of these teenagers he must have been sure were completely insane. As he exited, Sam entered, looking around at all of them curiously.

Meg smiled at Roxanne, relieved. "Well, if you think it's okay to be with Drew instead of my family . . ."

Roxanne rolled her eyes. "*Yes*, I think it's okay, okay? *Yes!*"

"Then let me ask you, let me ask all of you . . ." Meg turned, gesturing to encompass all three of her friends in the store. "I was thinking I'd make some signs for Drew's rally on Sunday. Do you think that's a good idea? I don't want to look too eager and maybe scare Drew off. Do you think I would?"

"Drew," Sam repeated, raising an eyebrow and looking at Luke. "That's the 'dating kind of guy,' right?"

"Don't ask me, I just work here," Luke mumbled.

Sam turned back to Meg. "What kind of rally is it?"

"We're protesting the university," Meg said

proudly, then shifted her tone to one of *Can you believe it?* outrage. "They want to kick black families out of their homes so the school can build a new science center!"

Sam nodded slowly and thoughtfully. "My cousin Willy's been talking about that a lot lately," he told them. "Lots of people are really upset about it."

"Aren't you?" Luke asked.

Sam shrugged. "I don't know yet," he confessed. "It doesn't sound so bad to me, those people getting out of that neighborhood and maybe starting fresh somewhere else."

"Come on," Luke shot back at Sam with a snort. "Do you really think that the university will give those families enough money to start over somewhere better than where they are now?"

Meg rushed over to the counter, and leaned across it eagerly, looking for advice. "So what do you think, Luke," she asked in a rush. "Should I make signs for the rally? I want him to know I'm interested and everything, but he's so smart, I'm worried he might know I'm *trying* to look interested, and then—"

Luke looked up abruptly, cutting her off, staring her square in the eye. "I thought the *cause* was what was important—those families and their homes, not impressing some . . . some *guy*. Which do care about more, Meg?"

Meg was so shocked by his outburst that she backed up a step or two from the counter. Sam looked at Luke in surprise, and even Roxanne turned to the conversation from the door. Meg could almost feel his anger like it was a solid thing he'd thrown at her, or a burst of heat from an oven whose door had fallen open. Luke *never* talked like that. It wasn't important what he had said, just the fact that he was so clearly, so obviously, angry with her.

"Luke," she stammered, "why are you . . ."

Luke looked away from her, slammed the register shut with a *clang,* and walked back to the record bins. "Nothing," he said. "Never mind. Do what you want."

Meg followed him, Roxanne a step or two behind. "Luke, what is it?"

"I said, never mind."

But Meg wouldn't let it go. "Why are you so upset, Luke? Tell me, really."

Luke paused, then turned to face her. Meg couldn't define his expression, because she'd never seen it before. It wasn't sadness, or anger, or frustration. It was some combination of the three.

"I'm upset because you're not thinking for yourself!" he told her. "You're smarter than this! I've spent lots of time talking to you, so I know! But you're just repeating everything this Drew guy has told you!"

Meg wanted to respond, wanted to get angry and yell back at Luke, but the words couldn't fly out of her throat. They were trapped down inside by the complete shock that someone other than her parents could talk to her like that. Not only were the words frozen, Meg was frozen too. She couldn't move an inch, immobilized by Luke's statements.

Roxanne, however, had no such problems. She peered at Luke from over Meg's shoulder. "Are you sure that's why you're upset?" she asked quietly.

A look passed between Roxanne and Luke, one that said each understood just what the other was saying. But Meg was still locked in place, trying to absorb everything that had just happened, letting the hurt wash over her, and never saw the exchange.

Luke dropped Roxanne's penetrating stare and turned back to the records. "I have stocking to do."

"But, but . . . ," Meg finally said, "Luke, what did you mean when—"

Roxanne gently took Meg's shoulder and pulled her to the door. "Don't worry about him," she urged. "Don't even think about him anymore. I've got something to take your mind off of it. *I* have a *real* problem!"

Roxanne tugged Meg along, past Sam, who could only watch, confused by everything that was happening. "Lenny's stood me up for another date today—again, for the third time," Rox told Meg. "And I need your help in figuring out what's going on!"

"Wait, Roxanne. Luke . . . ," Meg protested feebly.

"Roxanne, your shift isn't over," Luke called, not daring to look over at them.

"I'm taking my lunch break," Roxanne said, and with just enough of a trace of anger and menace that Luke didn't dare argue.

The door to the Vinyl Crocodile closed behind the girls, and they left the boys and the music behind as they stepped into the chilly air. As her ears filled with the sounds of traffic and other city noise, Meg at last felt the fog in her brain start to clear.

"What did he mean?" Meg wanted to know. "Roxanne, what did Luke mean?"

"Will you forget about Luke?" Rox pleaded. "Just come with me. Lenny's up to something, I know he is!"

Lenny Beeber lived in his grandmother's apartment in an old neighborhood populated almost entirely by elderly people. *Old people in old buildings,* Meg thought, although she knew that, in truth, *all* neighborhoods in Philadelphia were pretty old. The city had been around for more than two hundred years, after all.

Everywhere Meg looked along the streets of Lenny's neighborhood, there were people walking with canes or walkers. It seemed as though she had fallen through some sort of time portal, like in one of Will's comic books, and emerged in another universe where there were no teenagers, no adults, just old people.

It appeared to Meg as though there were tiny groceries on every corner that sold strange foods with names she had never heard, tons of shops and restaurants with words in unusual languages painted on the windows, lots of thrift stores and pawnshops. But it also seemed like everyone knew each other. The older people shuffled past one another, nodding and saying hello, frequently in accents Meg couldn't place.

Looking up, Meg could see that many apartment windows had fire escape gardens with small plants already starting to wilt in the newly cold weather, or cats perched on the sills inside, some sleeping, some looking out at the streets with detached curiosity. In a few windows, Meg could see old paintings hung on the walls, or yellowed photographs.

Roxanne had often wondered why Lenny would live in a neighborhood that was "so not-happening." Lenny, in return, had told her he figured the beauty and the benefits of it were simple: "Well, living with my grandmother, the rent's right. And all I have to do is change someone's light bulb now and then, or maybe help an old lady up the stairs with her groceries, and I've got free dinners for the next two weeks!"

But how could Lenny ever practice his bass? The people around here couldn't possibly approve of rock and roll. But Lenny had an answer for that, too. "I just keep my bass turned down really low," he had said. "Most of these folks, like my grandmother, don't hear so well anyway. And when I want to cut loose, I just take my gear over to a friend's, who lives in a more . . . understanding part of town."

As Meg and Rox walked past yet another corner

grocery, moving closer to Lenny's grandmother's apartment building, they met an elderly, sweet-faced woman coming the other way. She paused, looked up at Meg, and smiled, her face creased with enough lines to fill one of the giant maps Meg's father brought along on family vacations. The old woman said something that sounded like, "Share a pudding," and kept walking.

Meg turned around, surprised and confused. "What did she just say to me?"

"*Shayna punim,*" Roxanne answered, not turning around. "It means *pretty face* in Yiddish."

"In *what*-ish?"

"Yiddish."

"Is that supposed to be a language?"

"It *is* a language," Roxanne replied impatiently. "Sort of like Hebrew mixed with German mixed with Russian. Listen, don't worry about what language it is. I heard it maybe fifteen times when I first started coming down here. Trust me, she was giving you a compliment."

"Oh," Meg said, turning back around to call after the old lady. "Thank you!"

The old woman didn't answer—*She probably can't hear me,* Meg thought—so Meg turned her mind back to more pressing matters. "So, wait, tell me why you think Luke got so angry with me," she said.

Roxanne didn't even break stride. Since they'd left the Vinyl Crocodile, she'd been walking as fast as she possibly could, like someone determined to wear out the soles of her shoes. "Meg, will you just leave it alone?"

"How can I leave it alone?" Meg asked incredulously. "You heard all those things he said to me!"

Roxanne sighed. "He's probably just jealous."

"Jealous?" Meg couldn't believe it. It was as though Roxanne had just told her two plus two was, in fact, Chicago. "Luke? Jealous? That doesn't make any sense, Rox! It's not like I broke up with him! We both agreed it was the right thing to do. Why would Luke be jealous?"

Roxanne waved a hand impatiently at Meg, keeping her eyes pointed forward, as though staring with determination might somehow bring Lenny's building closer. "Can we talk about something *really* important for a second? I don't think you understand. Lenny's ditched me for"—her voice dropped low, as though Rox was tasting something unpleasant—"the *new girl*." Meg thought Roxanne would have spat on the sidewalk if she could have gotten away with it.

Meg hurried to keep up with her best friend. "And I still say you just have too much free time to think about stuff like this. Your imagination is running away with you!"

At last Roxanne stopped, and turned to face Meg. Meg hadn't realized it, but she was breathing heavily from walking so fast. "Lenny's the one who's running away," Rox said, with a definite tone of worry in her voice. "You won't believe what I found out about that girl!"

"She has a name," Meg reminded Rox. "Sherry Mann."

"'Sherry Mann.' Even the name sounds snooty," Roxanne said, with a worried tone.

Now Meg was worried, too. Usually Roxanne was her rock. Nothing bothered Roxanne Bojarski, and she had a plan to deal with any kind of situation. That always made Meg feel better about even the most dire problems. If Rox was worried, then something was really, truly wrong. "Snooty?" Meg wondered.

Roxanne nodded. "She just moved here from New York City."

Meg didn't know why *New York City* meant *snooty*, necessarily, but Meg knew Roxanne had a way of saving the worst information for last. Roxanne knew how to build up a big story.

"She's rich," Rox went on. "She's a year or two older than us, but her parents gave her her own car."

If that was true, Meg thought, then Sherry really *was* rich. In fact, she instantly became one of the richest people Meg knew. Meg couldn't even conceive of her parents giving her a car. In fact, these days, since the riots, it was hard for Meg to get her dad to let her leave the house.

But Roxanne wasn't finished there. "Get this: She's as big a music fan as I am. I heard she has more than two thousand records!"

Now that was *really* bad news. Roxanne prided herself on being the biggest music fan in Philadelphia. She knew Paul McCartney's middle name, what brand of guitar picks were preferred by Dave Davies of the Kinks, even what size shoe Mary Wilson wore. But even though Roxanne spent almost every dollar she had on records (or makeup, or clothes), she still couldn't afford to match someone like Sherry Mann album for album.

If Meg thought the bad news would end there, she was wrong. As usual, Rox had saved the absolute pinnacle of gloom for the finish. She barely choked out the words, looking down at the ground. "And Sherry broke up with her boyfriend just before she moved here . . . and he was a bass player!"

Meg gasped. "No!"

Roxanne shuffled over to a bus stop bench and sat down hopelessly. "It always happens this way," she moaned.

Meg sat down beside her, taking Rox's hands in a gesture of concerned support. "What always happens this way?"

"With musicians," Roxanne wailed. "When they get popular, girls just come out of the woodwork at them! Next thing you know, the musicians break up with their steady girlfriends, talking about how they have 'wild oats' they have to sow."

Meg had never understood that expression. She'd never seen anybody sowing wild oats, and she wasn't even sure what sowing was, nor had she ever seen a wild oat, to the best of her knowledge. She thought it had something to do with farming, but she didn't know of any musicians who liked farming. More likely, the saying was what Meg's English teacher would call a metaphor, but Meg still really wasn't sure what it was a metaphor for, and now wasn't the time to ask.

"Okay, you're way out of control," Meg said soothingly to Roxanne, patting her hands. "You've been reading too many sob stories in the magazines. Lenny's a great guy."

Roxanne shook her head. "Now he'll be great to someone else!"

"Look, I don't know Lenny very well," Meg admitted, helping Rox stand up. "But I do know he's not the kind of guy who would ever hurt you. Not ever."

Roxanne looked at her gratefully. "You think so? Really?"

"I know so," Meg replied, nodding firmly.

They started walking again, approaching the corner of Lenny's street. "You're right," Roxanne said, nodding to herself. "I'm just being silly. Lenny's my one and only, and I'm his. I don't know what I was thinking."

"See? That's the spirit," Meg encouraged as they turned the corner. But then Roxanne stopped abruptly in midstep, seeing something up ahead. Meg had to do a little dance step to avoid running into her friend. Meg looked in the same direction as Rox.

Stepping out the front door of Lenny's apartment building was Sherry Mann, in a pretty blue skirt and white sweater. Actually, *stepping* wasn't the right word. More accurately, Sherry was bouncing, as though she'd just had a particularly wonderful ride on a Ferris wheel, or heard that the Rolling Stones were going to be playing a concert in her backyard.

Parked at the curb was a new Ford that seemed to gleam even though the day was cloudy and there wasn't much sunlight. Sherry skipped around the front of the car and started to open the driver's side door. "Hey, Sherry," a familiar voice called out.

Sherry looked up to the source of the voice, and at the corner Meg and Roxanne did the same. They saw Lenny leaning out the window of his grandmother's fifth-floor apartment, smiling and waving down at Sherry. "I'll see you Sunday, right? One P.M.?"

Sherry waved back. "You know it, Lenster!"

Lenny ducked back through his window, closing it after him as Sherry started her car and pulled away. Meg couldn't believe what she'd just heard. "*Lenster?* Who calls anybody *Lenster?*"

Roxanne stared up at Lenny's window, in shock. Her voice was barely a whisper. "Sherry does," she said. "She probably calls him Beeber-Baby, too." She looked hopelessly at Meg. Meg had never seen Rox looking so sad. "That's what I call him, sometimes."

Seeing Rox like this almost made Meg want to cry. "Maybe it's not what it seems," she offered. "You should ask Lenny about it, get the story straight from him. You definitely should not jump to any conclusions."

But Meg could see that not only had Roxanne already jumped, she had fallen a very long way, and landed with a splat.

"What's the point?" she moaned. "I'll hear it from Lenny when he's ready to tell me. Ready to tell me he's breaking up with me for the . . . *new girl*."

Roxanne walked slowly back the way they came, her head down. Meg turned to watch her. An old woman, teetering the other direction on an old cane, smiled toothlessly at Meg. *"Shayna punim,"* she said.

This time, Meg couldn't even say thank you.

Seven

Home after school on Tuesday, Meg opened the front door as quietly as she could, and closed it behind her. She lay the four long pieces of wood and squares of poster board she'd bought at the hardware store behind the coat rack. Then she carefully tiptoed through her house. She was pretty sure no one would be home, but she wanted to make sure.

Her father was certainly at his store, Pryor TV and Radio, working with Sam Walker's father, Henry, to sell the latest in black-and-white consoles or hi-fi stereo systems. The store wouldn't close for the day until six.

Her mother was supposed to have taken off work from her job at the travel agency early in order to bring Will to yet another doctor for yet another "second opinion." At some point, Meg believed, they should stop calling it a second opinion. By now, according to her calculations, they were on the seventh opinion. And Will still didn't know any more about what was going to be happening to him. It didn't seem fair.

Patty, meanwhile, was probably at the library. It was her custom to go there after school any day she could. Patty certainly enjoyed the library, Meg knew, but there was also the fact that Patty didn't really have any friends to hang out with after school the way Meg had Roxanne. Patty's intelligence set her apart from girls her own age, and not in a way that helped her socially. Meg knew that was why Patty was so interested in everything Meg did with Roxanne—she was fascinated by the concept of even having a best friend. Meg felt a little bad for her little sister once in a while, but even understanding why Patty did what she did didn't make her sister's nosiness less annoying.

There shouldn't be anyone home at all. But as she approached the living room, she heard a voice.

She wasn't alone in the house.

Meg's heart skipped a beat. The door had been locked when she'd come in. But that didn't mean that, somewhere in the back of the house, a window hadn't been broken, or the back door crashed in.

Meg tensed and listened. The voice was too low to be heard clearly, but it didn't sound like an angry voice. Then again, it didn't sound like anyone in her family, either.

She knew what she her father would tell her to do. "Don't fool around, Meg," he'd say. "Get out of the house, go across the street to the Hamptons' or the Palisettis', and tell them to call the police."

What she knew she shouldn't do is creep closer to the living room with the intention of peeking around the doorway to get a glimpse of the intruder. But that's exactly what Meg found herself doing. She moved closer and closer, trying desperately to keep the soles of her penny loafers from making any noise on the floor, her heart pounding. The voice kept its same low tone. Meg tried not to imagine the worst possible scenario—masked burglars stealing everything that was valuable to her family—and kept moving forward.

Finally she reached the edge of the doorway. Taking a deep breath, she turned her body around, then leaned inch by inch to the side so her eye just peeked little by little around the edge. The living room revealed itself to her in sections: There was no one on the couch. There was no one in her father's chair. There was no one looking out the window. There was no one watching the TV, which showed a weatherman giving the forecast for the next few days.

The TV was on!

Meg sagged back against the wall, her held breath hissing out of her in relief. Will must have left the television on when he and their mother had left for the doctor's office.

Chuckling at herself for getting so worked up, Meg walked into the empty living room and shut the television off. All this sneaking around was starting to get to her. She'd be happy when Sunday had come and gone, and she wouldn't have the secret of Drew's protest to keep from her parents. Meg took another deep breath in the welcome silence of the house, all tension slipping away.

Then the doorbell rang!

So unexpected was the noise, Meg actually screamed, pressing her fists to her mouth like she was an extra in a horror movie and had just seen the Wolfman crash through her window. A chill raced up her spine and back down before her frantic thoughts finally slowed down, and she was able to identify the noise.

Someone's at the door, Meg reassured herself. Feeling extra stupid, she smoothed her blouse, cleared her throat, and walked to the front of the house. She paused, glancing at the wood and poster board, wondering if maybe she should shove them into a closet, then decided against it. Whoever had come to visit wasn't part of her family, obviously, and they were the only ones who would demand an explanation.

Meg stood on tiptoes to look through the pane of glass at the top of the door, and saw Sam Walker waiting on the stoop, holding a brown paper bag. Puzzled, Meg unlatched the door and opened it. "Sam? What are you doing here?" Meg wanted to know.

Sam looked as surprised to see her as she was to see him. He was still wearing his East Catholic High jacket, just as she was still wearing her own school uniform. He must have come right from his last class. "I didn't think you'd be home. I thought you'd be at the record store or something."

Meg smiled wearily. "Yeah, well, the record store hasn't been the most fun place for me, lately."

Sam nodded in understanding. "Yeah."

Meg opened the door wider. "Come on in."

Sam looked around uncertainly, and Meg knew why. Though there was nothing wrong, legally or any other way, with a black teenage boy going into a white girl's house, there were still lots of people, unfortunately, who felt otherwise. Even Meg's parents, who were friendly with the Walkers, might have trouble with the idea, particularly when they weren't home with Meg. There was still an unspoken set of rules that both whites and blacks were aware of, lines that neither side felt comfortable approaching. It was better than it used to be; her father had told her stories of separate water fountains for blacks, as well as restaurants and many other things, not that long ago—but it still wasn't perfect.

The unspoken rules sometimes made Meg angry, as she knew they would make Drew angry. Henry Walker had worked with Meg's father for more than a decade. He and his children were practically members of the Pryors' extended family. Sam and Meg had grown up together, albeit in very different economic circumstances and different neighborhoods. He was her friend, and she had no problem with opening the door to her family's home to him. However, Meg also understood why Sam might have trouble walking inside.

"Just for a minute," he finally said, stepping past her into the living room. Meg closed the door behind him.

Sam looked around, and saw the wood and poster board behind the coat rack. "You decided to make the signs, huh?"

Meg blushed a little. "Yeah. Roxanne always says, you've got to take your chances."

Sam nodded, then paused thoughtfully. "Luke sounded kind of upset the other day."

Meg sat down on the couch. "I'm not really sure what's going on there. Roxanne thinks maybe Luke is jealous."

"He didn't seem like it before. When you first broke up."

"I know, that's what makes it so weird. That, plus Luke got really steamed about me helping Drew with the rally, like I'm some puppet for Drew or something! Sam, you don't think that's true, do you?"

Sam thought about it for a moment. "I've never seen the two of you together, so I don't really know."

That wasn't the answer Meg wanted to hear. Meg wanted Sam to tell her that of course she wasn't Drew's puppet. That Meg was smart and could make her own choices, and that's what she'd done, she'd chosen Drew. Anger flared in her toward Sam for just a second, because he wasn't giving her the support she wanted, but then it subsided as quickly as it came. Sam was being honest with her. It was the thing she appreciated most about their friendship. He would always tell her the truth about what he was thinking, whether it was what she wanted to hear or not. She could count on him for that.

Suddenly, Meg remembered that Sam was holding a paper bag. "What's that?" she asked.

Sam looked down at the bag in surprise. He had forgotten all about it, too. "Oh. It's a casserole dish," he said. "Your mother brought it over after my mother . . ." His voice trailed off to nothing, then he seemed to shake himself out of it. "I had it in my locker at school all day today, and kept meaning to give it back, but I never ran into you."

Meg instantly felt terrible. Here she had been running off at the mouth about her boy problems, even getting angry with Sam for not saying exactly the right things, when he was still dealing with the recent death of his mother. Meg couldn't imagine the kind of pain Sam had been in, and despite her earlier reminder to herself to be more of a friend to Sam, she hadn't done it.

"Sam, I'm so sorry," she said, unsure of what to say next. "I hope you're doing all right" was the best she could muster.

Sam shrugged and looked away from her. "I'm okay, I guess," he said quietly.

"You father . . . your sister . . ."

"They're doing the best they can. It's hardest on my sister," he said quietly. "She keeps coming home from school, thinking our mother's going to be there, but . . ." Meg could tell from the sound of his voice that his sister wasn't the only one having a difficult time with the change in their family.

Meg looked down at her hands, then back up at Sam. "Sam, I really am sorry. I've been an awful friend to you through this."

Sam smiled. "You've got your own stuff going on," he said. "You and your family have been real good to me and mine."

"I'm just saying, if you ever want to talk . . ."

Sam nodded gratefully. "Thanks." There was a long pause, then Sam said, "I should probably get going."

Meg walked him back to the door. Sam set the bag he was carrying on the front hall table. "I'll see you at the record store?" he asked.

"More likely at school," Meg replied, thinking of Luke.

"Don't let it bother you so much," Sam suggested. "It sounds like Luke's the one with the problem, so let him deal with it."

Meg smiled. "That sounds like good advice," she said. "Thanks, Sam."

He smiled and gave a little wave, walking out and down the stoop. Meg watched him go, happy that he had come by, and closed the door.

Meg was at last alone, but she knew she didn't have as much time remaining to her before her family got home as she had before. Quickly, she went into the garage and rummaged through the shelves of her father's hardware supplies, finally finding what she wanted: three cans of different-colored paint, a screwdriver to open them with, a hammer and four nails, and three thick paint-brushes. Hopefully all of the things she took had been from far enough back on the shelves that, even if her father came home before she had a chance to return everything, he wouldn't notice anything was missing.

Meg went back into the house with the paint, brushes, hammer, nails, and screwdriver, stopped at the front door to pick up the wood and poster board, and then, her arms full, struggled up the stairs to her attic room.

She closed the door behind her, dumped all of her materials on the floor, and kicked off her shoes. As she sat down and arranged her supplies, Meg's thoughts turned back to Roxanne. Meg had never seen her best friend so upset. If that was what being in love could lead to, Meg wasn't sure she wanted to let her feelings ever get that far for anyone. Then again, she reasoned, love meant highs and lows— when it was bad, it was very bad, but when it was good, it had to be incredible. Thinking about those highs, perhaps with Drew, made love seem worthwhile to Meg.

Cheered, she used the screwdriver to pry open the lid of a half-empty can of her father's blue paint and stirred it gently with a paintbrush. Inspiration struck her, and she grabbed a stack of teen magazines from next to her bed. She had read them all three times each, so it made sense to put them to good use now. Meg spread them out underneath the cans of paint and the poster board. All it would take was one drop of paint on the floor for her mother or father to start asking questions, and then Meg would *really* be in trouble.

Meg thought about putting a record on to keep her company, then decided against it. She wanted to be able to hear her family if they happened to come home. That way, she'd have time to stash the signs she was going to make under her bed.

With everything properly laid out, Meg dipped the brush into the paint and moved it to the first piece of poster board, spattering a few drops of blue onto magazine photos of John, Paul, George, and Ringo as she did. Carefully, she painted a graceful *S* onto the board. She wrote SAVE THIS NEIGHBORHOOD cleanly and clearly, although she'd miscalculated the space necessary for the last word and the letters got slightly bunched together at the end. Meg shrugged. It was good enough. She took another brush, dipped its edge in red paint, and outlined the blue letters.

Meg gently laid the freshly painted poster board atop one of the pieces of wood so that the wood ran down the back center of the sign. Then she took a nail, carefully held it over the center of the sign, and hammered it into the wood. Then she waved it experimentally above her head. It flapped about a bit, but held firm. *Not bad,* Meg thought.

Meg put the sign back down, and prepared to make another. But just as she picked up the paintbrush, her door opened.

Meg scrambled to hide the signs, and nearly knocked over the can of blue paint. The pieces of wood clattered together, and the hammer fell from her lap with a loud *thud.* There was no point in trying to hide anymore. Whoever was coming in had no doubt heard the commotion. All Meg could do was wait for the yelling to begin.

But, to her surprise, the face that peeked around the door wasn't her mother or her father, but Patty. And Patty looked as surprised as Meg felt. She quickly started to close the door.

"Hey!" Meg shouted, and Patty froze, peeking back in. "What are you doing, Patty?"

"I . . . I didn't think you were home," her younger sister replied.

"So that would have made it okay for you to come in my room? Do you do that a lot when I'm not home?"

"No," Patty replied, then looked away. "Hardly ever." Then she saw the signs and paint before Meg and frowned. "What are you doing?"

Meg tried to cover the supplies before her. "None of your business, and don't try to change the subject! Is Mom home, too?"

Patty shook her head, still looking at the one sign Meg had completed. "'Save This Neighborhood'? What does that mean?"

"I said it was none of your business," Meg growled.

Patty's eyes grew mischievous. "Is it Mom's business? Because I could ask her about it if you don't feel like telling me." She started again to close the door.

"Patty, wait," Meg pleaded, reaching out from where she sat. The door froze again and Patty looked back inside with an innocent smile. "You can't tell Mom."

"Really? Why can't I?"

Meg sighed. "I'll do your chores for a week."

"A week?" Patty yelped incredulously. "That's hardly anything! Keeping a secret is worth a month of chores, at least!"

"*Two* weeks," Meg offered.

"It's a deal," Patty chirped, walking into the room.

Meg rolled her eyes. "Close the door, will you?"

Patty closed the door behind her. "So, is this why you're really not going to the movies with us on Sunday?"

Meg looked up at her sister, startled, and now it was Patty's turn to roll her eyes. "Please," Patty said. "It was so obvious you weren't telling the whole truth."

"Do you think Mom and Dad knew?" Meg asked, worried.

"Probably," Patty answered with a shrug.

Meg frowned. "Then why didn't they say anything about it?"

Patty shrugged again, more interested in the

signs. "So, what's 'Save This Neighborhood' all about?"

"I'm helping students at Penn protest the university," Meg explained.

"Why? What's the university doing?" Patty wanted to know.

"They want to kick people out of their homes so the school can build a new science center where they've been living."

Patty's eyes grew wide. "They're actually going to kick people out?"

"Well, no," Meg told her. "The school's going to pay people for their houses."

Patty frowned, puzzled. "So the people *aren't* being kicked out? They can say no, if they want to?"

"I suppose, but—"

"What are they going to be studying at the science center?"

"It could be some bad stuff," Meg told her sister. She couldn't remember exactly what Drew had told her, only how his eyes had looked when he'd said it.

"But it could be some good stuff?"

Meg felt herself growing frustrated with Patty's questions, mostly because she didn't really know the answers. And that made her think back to what Luke had said, about how Meg was only repeating things Drew had told her without thinking, without coming up with opinions and perspectives on her own. Meg angrily stepped on her thoughts about Luke and thrust a paintbrush out to her sister. It was easier to paint—and more fun to think about Drew—than it was to worry about what her ex-boyfriend thought. "Never mind, Patty, just paint!"

Patty took the brush. "What should I paint?"

"I don't know, anything."

Patty thought about it, tapping the handle of the brush against her chin. "How about . . . 'Families Can't Live in a Science Center.'"

Meg looked up. "That's pretty good," she admitted. "I'll paint that, you think of another one."

Patty shrugged, and the two girls bent over their signs, their brushes moving carefully. Meg enjoyed the quiet, and found herself enjoying working alongside Patty. She really wasn't so bad when she wasn't talking all the time. And it was nice to work on a project, sister and sister. But Meg made a mental note not to let Patty ever know she felt that way. Patty would never let her hear the end of it.

Meg glanced over at Patty's sign. It read, HOMES, SWEET HOMES. That was pretty good, too. Patty was a natural at this. Meg hid a small smile, and went back to painting the *C* in *science center*. And then the door to her room opened a second time.

Now Meg *and* Patty scrambled to hide the signs. Both reached for the hammer, and—*klunk*—knocked heads painfully. "Ow!" they cried out at the same time.

Will poked his head around the door. "What happened?" he asked.

Meg rubbed the sore spot on her forehead. "Doesn't anybody *knock* in this house?" she wondered grumpily.

Will limped into the room and closed the door behind him. "What happened?" he asked again.

"What are you doing in here?" Meg demanded to know.

"I saw Patty's book bag downstairs, so I knew she was home," Will explained.

Meg didn't get it. "You saw her book bag, okay, but how did you know she was up in *my* room?"

"Patty's always in your room when you're not home," Will answered with a shrug.

Meg turned a scowl on her sister, who glared at Will. "Way to go, Will! I thought we agreed you weren't going to say anything!"

Will grimaced, embarrassed. "Oh yeah, I forgot." He turned to Meg. "I meant to say, I *guessed* Patty was in here."

Patty turned to Meg and smiled innocently. Meg rolled her eyes. "Forget it!"

Will looked at the signs. "What are you doing?"

Meg hammered a nail into one of the finished signs as quietly as she could. If Will was home, their mother was, too, so the less noise they made, the better. "We're making signs. And you can't tell Mom and Dad."

Will smiled. "I won't, if you promise to do my chores for—"

"Hey," Meg interrupted, angry. "I'm not doing chores for anybody! If either of you tell Mom or Dad, then I'll tell them I caught you sneaking into my room!"

Will's smile vanished. "I won't tell," he quickly promised. Patty nodded in agreement.

Silence returned to the room, and Will watched his sisters paint. After a moment, Patty looked up at him. "How did it go at the doctor's?" she asked. It was a different tone of voice than Patty usually used, Meg thought. It had more worry to it, more concern. Meg knew Patty genuinely felt bad that Will didn't really understand the operation their parents were considering to correct his polio. Meg didn't understand it either, to tell the truth, but she thought that the person who was about to have an operation should know a little something about it. But it wasn't up to Meg or Patty to tell Will. Their parents would do that, when they felt the time was right.

Will shrugged as if it didn't matter, but Meg could hear the fear in his voice, barely hidden. "The doctor used a needle to get some of my blood—it didn't hurt as much as last time—and he tried to bend my leg a couple different ways. Then he and Mom talked for a while." He looked up from the sign to Patty. "What does *concur* mean?"

"It means *agree*," Patty told him quietly.

"That's what the doctor said to Mom," Will said. "He said he concurred with what the other doctors have told her."

Meg and Patty nodded, looking sympathetically at their little brother. "That's good, Will," Meg assured him. "It's always better to concur than not to concur." Meg wasn't even sure if that was always true, but she hoped it made Will feel better.

"I guess that means I'm definitely going to have an operation," Will said with a weary sigh.

"I don't know," Meg answered honestly.

Will shook himself a little, as if almost physically forcing himself to change the subject. He looked down at the signs again. "What do those say?"

"We're making signs to protest the university's new science center," Patty told him.

Will smiled brightly. "I like science," he said eagerly.

"This isn't the good kind of science," Meg explained.

Will shrugged. "Can I help paint?"

"We're actually almost done," Meg said, hammering a nail into the last sign. Then she saw the look of disappointment on Will's face. "You can help us put the lids back on the paint and clean up, though." She thought about it, then added, "If you don't ask any more questions."

Will smiled agreeably. "Okay," he said. He struggled into a sitting position, stretching out his braced leg in front of him on the floor, and picked up the lid to the blue paint can. As he set about replacing it on the can, Meg and Patty looked at each other and shared a rare smile.

Later, with the signs safely hidden under Meg's bed, Meg and Patty craftily replaced the painting supplies in the garage while their mother prepared dinner and their father changed out of his work clothes.

Dinner for the family was mostly silent. Uncle Pete, who usually had more than a few good stories from his daily patrols, had a late shift and couldn't come over. Meg spent the meal wondering just how mad her father still was at her, and why he hadn't yelled at her more about not spending Sunday afternoon with the family. She thought about Luke's anger, and her own excitement about seeing Drew again on Saturday, when she'd bring the signs to him on campus. And she thought how small her concerns felt in the face of Sam's troubles, or even Will's.

A few hours later, taking a break from homework, Meg walked into the kitchen and found her parents there, finishing JJ's care package. Meg's mom held the top flaps of the cardboard box down while her father ran packaging tape down the seam, sealing it. Both of her parents looked up at Meg as she came in. They held her eyes for a moment; then her mother reached for a ball of twine to tie off the package as her father leaned back against the kitchen counter.

"Meg, your mother and I have discussed your plans for the weekend," he said to her, then looked at his wife. Something in their look made Meg think their discussion may not have been the most pleasant conversation ever.

"Yes?" Meg asked warily.

"And I've decided you don't have to come with us to see the movie," her dad finished.

Meg heaved a huge inward sigh of relief. She'd been wondering what she would do if her father had told her she couldn't go. Would she have sneaked away from her family in the middle of the movie? Would she have faked illness so she could stay home, then go be with Drew after her family left? As bad as Meg felt for not wanting to be with her family, being that deceptive would have made it a hundred times worse. Now, she didn't have to feel guilty—about that, at least.

"I trust you completely," Jack Pryor continued, looking Meg squarely in the eye. "And I believe that, since you'll be with Beth the entire time, you'll be totally safe and looked-after."

Something about the way her father was looking at her made Meg very uncomfortable. His eyes were like searchlights, looking for the buried treasure of a hidden secret. *He knows,* she thought, trying not to let her face show it. *But he's letting me go. Why?* The question made her feel even more nervous, and more guilty.

Her dad never looked away from her. "I know you won't do anything foolish or put yourself in danger." He crossed the few steps across the kitchen floor and put his hand on her shoulder. "I know, because I trust you." And then, finally, he looked away from Meg and walked out of the kitchen.

"Thank you," Meg called quietly to him as he walked out.

Meg's mother picked up the care package, smiled at Meg, and followed her husband into the living room.

Meg stood where she was for a long moment, still feeling her father's hand on her shoulder. Part of her wanted to run into the living room and tell her parents everything. But instead, she went to the refrigerator and poured herself a glass of cold milk to drown her guilty feelings.

Eight

For Meg, Friday was mostly a matter of counting the minutes until the end of the school day, whereupon she'd start counting the minutes until midnight, and then the moments until she'd pay her surprise visit to Drew on Saturday. All week long, she had thought about the signs she'd made, and how Drew might react when he saw them. The lessons dragged on and on until, finally, Meg looked over at Roxanne during their third period, hoping for a sympathetic face. Instead, Roxanne stared miserably out the window. Meg decided she couldn't let her friend's sad mood stand any longer.

When the bell rang, Meg dragged Rox into the girls' room. Roxanne went along without protest, as though she were too tired or too weak to put up a fight. "Roxanne," Meg begged, "you've got to snap out of it!"

"You sound like Luke," Roxanne grumbled. "Why do I have to snap out of anything?"

"Because this isn't like the Roxanne Bojarski I know!"

"This is the new Roxanne Bojarski, the one who got dumped by her boyfriend."

Meg frowned, angry. "Lenny hasn't dumped you! You haven't even talked to him about it, have you?"

Roxanne looked at herself in the bathroom mirror, depressed. "No."

Meg turned her friend around. "The Roxanne Bojarski I know doesn't quit. She'd fight for her boyfriend."

Tears welled in Rox's eyes. "Sherry Mann's everything I'm not, Meg! She's beautiful, she's rich—"

"Okay, first of all, *you're* just as beautiful," Meg said, cutting her best friend off. "Even little old ladies call you 'share a pudding'!"

"*Shayna punim,*" Rox said, correcting her.

"Whatever! Second, money doesn't mean anything to Lenny! And third, who came up with the plan to get us on *Bandstand*?"

Rox sniffled, then murmured, "I did."

"Who got us in to see Martha Reeves and the Vandellas just by smiling at the usher?"

Rox looked up, her voice a little stronger. "I did."

"Who shortened the hem of her school uniform skirt by a sixteenth of an inch every month for four months so that the nuns wouldn't even notice? And now we've all done it! Who started that trend?"

"I did."

"The Roxanne Bojarski who did all those things may lose her boyfriend, but she's not going to do it because she's hiding in a bathroom crying her eyes out!"

Roxanne wiped a hand across her eyes, a look of determination moving onto her face. "You're right. You're right, Meg." She smiled, and the two girls hugged. Roxanne laughed. "That's twice in one week you've been the one giving me good advice. That's a new record!"

Meg joined her friend in laughing. They had both done too little of it lately.

The next day, finally, was Saturday, and it dawned crisp and clear. "A good day for the Irish," JJ would have called it. JJ was a die-hard college football fan, particularly for the Notre Dame Fighting Irish, who would be playing on a beautiful fall afternoon like this. JJ had been headed to Notre Dame himself, hoping to play football, before he had injured his ankle in high school and been forced to rethink his future. Now he was hundreds of miles away in marine boot camp, and soon he might very well be even farther away than that.

Meg shook such thoughts away as she walked across the Penn campus, carrying her signs. A couple students had looked curiously at Meg, and her signs, since she'd gotten off the crosstown bus, cocking their heads to the side to try and read what was written on the placards. Meg hadn't slowed to let them read, hadn't even acknowledged their looks, choosing instead to walk on proudly, head high, on a mission of great importance.

These signs were important to Drew's cause. No, they were *crucial*, and as soon as Drew would see them, he'd be amazed by how seriously Meg was taking the issue, how deeply she wanted to be involved. He'd look at her in a new way, as someone who connected with him on the levels that were most important to him. He'd start to think of her as more than just a high school girl with a crush, and maybe he'd see her as a *partner*, and they'd spend long hours sitting on the floor of his dorm room, staring into each other's eyes. Drew would tell Meg all of his dreams about how to change the world for the better, and Meg would think of ways she could help. They'd be the perfect team.

But suddenly, Meg was struck by a vision of herself arriving outside the door to Drew's dorm, only to see a pretty coed leaving, and Drew leaning out his window to say good-bye, much like she'd seen Lenny do earlier in the week. Meg could never forget the hurt in Roxanne's eyes, or her voice. It made Meg a little scared to feel so strongly about someone, knowing there was a possibility she could end up in so much pain.

Meg quickened her pace toward Drew's dorm, as though she were in a hurry to see her very own "new girl," as Roxanne had put it. She got about ten steps before she tripped over a piece of uneven sidewalk. She didn't fall, but in keeping her balance, the signs fell from her arms, scattering across the concrete with a clatter. Embarrassed, she avoided the amused looks of the students around her—*Crazy high school girl*, Meg imagined them thinking—and scooped up the signs once more before continuing on her way.

Meg arrived at the dorm a few moments later, and was most relieved to not see any pretty young college girls waving back over their shoulders at Drew smiling out the window at them. But then she realized that might only mean that the "new girl" was still *in* Drew's room!

Meg hurried into the dorm, up the stairs, and down the hall to Drew's room. Halfway down, she suddenly stopped, causing a surprised student behind her to nimbly dodge around. He walked past, looking grumpily over his shoulder at her.

I'm being stupid, Meg thought. *Drew and I aren't exclusive. We're not even anything, I guess. But he doesn't have a girl in his room. He's going to see my signs, he's going to be thrilled, and everything's going to be just perfect.*

But a little flicker of doubt remained in Meg's heart as she took the last few steps down the hall to Drew's door. She could see it was open a crack, with a book propping it open. Her heart skipped a beat. The first time she'd been alone with Drew in his room, he'd used a book to keep the door open, because the school's rule was that if a boy had a girl in his room, he had to leave the door open the width of a book.

And now Meg could hear a voice coming from the room, a girl's voice. It sounded like the girl Meg had met with Drew a few days before, Natalie. But Meg couldn't hear what she was saying. And Meg didn't care. She just wanted to get this over with. Shifting the signs into one arm, she used the other to push the door open, prepared for the worst.

Instead, she saw, as the door swung open, Drew sitting on his bed, Natalie and Dan and Greg sitting on the floor, and Cliff sitting in the desk chair. None of them even looked up as the door opened. "That's just naive," Cliff was saying, shaking his head at Natalie. "We're *not* being taken seriously. As far as the school's concerned, we're still just a bunch of loudmouthed kids!"

Drew made a calming gesture with both hands. "Okay, okay, we're not going to get anywhere by arguing with each other, Cliff, just settle down."

Cliff scowled. "I'm getting tired of you telling me that, Mandel! We're not going to get anywhere by sitting around the dorm, either!"

"We haven't been sitting around the dorm, Cliff," Greg reminded him, a weary edge to his voice. "We've been getting out and doing lots of things lately."

"Not fast enough for my tastes," Cliff grumped, folding his arms across his chest.

"Hi," Meg said quietly. On the one hand, she was incredibly relieved to find that Drew wasn't alone in his room with another girl, as she'd feared. On the other hand, however, Drew wasn't alone and waiting for her to arrive and brighten his life, as she'd hoped. There would be no brilliant moment between them, no start of an exciting new chapter.

Drew looked over at the sound of her voice. "Oh,

hi, High School," he said, a slight frown on his face. Meg knew the frown was a lingering effect of Cliff's comment, but it wasn't the smile she would have preferred. And there he was, calling her "High School" again, another reminder of the age difference between them; another reminder, whether he intended it or not, that they weren't partners, they weren't on the same level. "Sorry, we were talking. Come on in, and close the door again, would you?" He turned back to Cliff. "We're going out tomorrow to confront more property assessors, remember?"

Meg stood still in the doorway for a moment, as though waiting for Drew to say something more to her. When he didn't, Meg stepped into the room and quietly closed the door. She looked for a place to set down the signs and, finding none, leaned them against the door, then sat on the floor next to Dan.

"Big deal," Cliff shot back at Drew. "We're going to gab at a bunch of guys in suits. Is that going to change anything? Is that going to keep the school from kicking those people out of their houses? Maybe we slow them down for a little while, but we're just annoying them, not accomplishing anything! To them, we're just a bunch of spoiled kids with not enough homework to do!"

Drew stood up to make his next point. "I absolutely disagree," Drew replied. "We're effecting change in a mature, professional manner that shows we're serious."

Cliff stood up as well, coming nose to nose with Drew. "Serious? Serious isn't just blocking some assessors on the street, making it harder for them to walk around us, which they're going to do a minute and a half later!"

Cliff's face was so red, Meg felt sure his next move would be to take a swing at Drew, but neither Natalie, Greg, nor Dan looked like they were going to get involved. Meg knew she couldn't let anything happen. "I brought signs," she blurted out, gesturing frantically to where they lay against the door. "I thought they might be good for tomorrow!"

Cliff gave Drew one last sour look, then walked past Meg to the door, picking up one of the signs. "Save This Neighborhood," he read, then snorted. "Brilliant."

Drew pushed past Meg and took the sign from Cliff. "It's great, Meg," he said, turning his back on Cliff. "We really appreciate it."

"Yeah," Cliff said sarcastically over Drew's shoulder. "Signs are just what we've been missing.

Signs will definitely take our protests to the next level!"

Drew spun on Cliff. "And what do you think really *will* take our protests to the 'next level,' Cliff? Beating up those assessors?"

Cliff put his hands on his hips and tipped his chin up in the air. "Absolutely," he said. "If things go that far, I think we should let it. That'll show we don't intend to back down on any cause for any reason!"

"No. That's one hundred percent wrong," Drew replied. "If we want to be a lasting and legitimate voice in the battle for social change, we're going to do it from within the existing system!"

This definitely wasn't going the way Meg had hoped. Not only was she apparently not going to get to share a personal moment with Drew—he had barely noticed the signs she had worked so hard on—there was no way she could break things up if Drew and Cliff got into a fistfight. And she wasn't really sure what they were fighting over, anyway.

"I'm going to go," she said, interrupting the heated exchange between the two boys. "I just remembered, I have to help my mother do the grocery shopping for dinner tonight . . ." She shouldered past Cliff and Drew, opened the door, knocking over the rest of the signs, and stepped out into the hall.

Meg hurried toward the stairs, wrestling with her emotions. Part of her wanted to stay by Drew's side and help him drive off Cliff's challenge. But another part of her didn't want to be around if she couldn't be the focus of Drew's attention. She wondered if he even wanted her around for tomorrow. But Meg also had to sigh inwardly. There was some small consolation to be taken from the afternoon's encounter. After all, it certainly seemed like the last thing Drew was interested in was having a girl in his room other than Meg, or any girl, for that matter.

Meg had nearly reached the stairs when she heard Drew's voice call out from behind her. "Meg!"

She turned around to see Drew running down the hall. His hair flopped as he ran, his T-shirt was untucked, and he carried one of her signs. Meg had to smile. He looked cute. "You don't really have to leave," he said, slightly out of breath from his run.

Meg looked down at the ground. "I really do. My mom is expecting me."

He held up the sign. "These are really great. Really."

"Thanks."

He spun the sign in his hand, trying to think of

what to say next. "I'm very sorry about that, back there," he apologized, pointing down the hall to his dorm room door. "Cliff can get me riled up, but we need his energy. He's really committed."

"I understand," Meg told him, half meaning it. As far as she was concerned, having someone as hot-tempered as Cliff around couldn't be good for any cause.

"You're coming back tomorrow, right?"

Meg looked at him seriously. "Do you want me to?"

He looked back into her eyes, his expression absolutely serious. Meg felt her whole body tingle. "Absolutely."

Now Meg was a little out of breath herself. "Then I'll be there."

Drew's smile lit the hallway even brighter. "I'm already looking forward to seeing you," he said. He leaned in to kiss her, but just as he did, the dorm room door nearest them opened, and a student stepped out, carrying a basket of laundry. Drew hastily pulled back, smiled, and blushed. Meg was left leaning slightly forward in anticipation of the kiss. She regained her balance and smiled back at Drew.

He walked backward down the hall, holding the

sign up again. "Thanks again for these. They're perfect."

Meg waved good-bye. "See you tomorrow," she said.

Drew gave her one last smile and disappeared back into his room. Meg turned back to the stairs and started down. Whereas the tingle she felt from Drew's previous kisses had been enough to last her days, the brief thrill of this almost-kiss vanished with every step she took. Meg knew she wasn't at the top of Drew's list of priorities . . . and maybe she wasn't ever going to be.

On her way home, Meg, still troubled, got off the bus a few stops early, and walked across the street to Vinyl Crocodile. Under normal circumstances, the record store was her favorite place to go when she had big problems on her mind, not because she could think more easily there, but because there was something comforting to flipping through racks of records, even if they were records she had looked through many times before. The routine was peaceful, and she loved being around the music in any way she could, letting the songs from the store's hi-fi wash over her as she memorized the names of tunes and the pictures of bands from the record sleeves.

Her mother and father would never want to hear her say such a thing, but more than once, Meg had thought that perhaps she felt the same way about the record store that they felt about church. It was a place where she could focus, relax, and be completely comfortable. The record store was a place where she could just *be*.

Of course, it had become less enjoyable to be in Vinyl Crocodile since Luke had started acting so strangely. These days, Meg was of two minds when it came to Luke. She wanted to see him, but she didn't want to see him. She didn't want to argue with him or have him attack her, but she also wanted to clear the air between them, and she knew that would probably mean a fight of some kind. But it didn't matter today—she *needed* Vinyl Crocodile.

Meg walked into the store and, as casually as she could, looked around for Luke. She couldn't see him. *He must be in the stockroom for a second,* she thought. Nobody was in the listening booths, either, and Meg was sad for that. Sam would be a good person to talk to right now, she knew. Even if he didn't have any advice for what she could do with Luke, he'd at least listen to her, and maybe that was what she needed most.

Meg moved to the record racks and started shuffling through them. Naturally they hadn't changed since the last time she'd been in. On the store stereo, Nancy Sinatra was singing. She always sounded sad to Meg, even when singing faster-moving, angrier songs like her biggest hit, "These Boots Are Made for Walking."

Meg heard the door to the stockroom open, and turned quickly to look. Luke was closing the door behind him. Meg turned back around, wishing quietly that he'd notice her, come over, and ask what was wrong. Maybe he'd even apologize for how he'd been behaving.

She heard footsteps behind her and caught her breath. "Meg," Luke said.

"Yes?" she answered without looking at him.

"I have something for you."

Meg turned around, ready for an apology, perhaps, or even flowers. But instead all she saw was Luke looking serious, glasses perched on his nose. "I was going to bring these by your house later, maybe leave them in the mailbox." He had a small stack of papers in his hand. "I got curious about that science center thing you've been doing, so I looked into it."

Meg leaned back against the record racks. This

wasn't what she had hoped for at all. "Oh?" she said. "Really?"

Luke looked a little embarrassed. "I found a list of potential tenants the university is considering for the center, if they ever get it built. It's easy to find these things, actually, if you're willing to go to enough offices and ask enough questions."

Meg stood where she was, trying hard not to change her expression. But in her head, her thoughts were whirling. Was Luke checking up on the science center just so he could attack her again? Or was there some other reason?

"Anyway," Luke went on, clearing his throat at her silence, "I thought you might be interested. And I circled one I thought might really mean something to you."

He held the list out to Meg, and she took it from him, looking down at the pages. Archimedes Engineering. Doctors Robert Fairweather and Marcel Lemieux. The Exeter Corporation. And many others. Meg had never heard of any of them, and many of them specialized in sciences or studies she had never heard of, like paleobiology and psychobiology. She didn't see anything that looked military, or had a name like Project Spice Rack, as Drew and Cliff and their friends had feared. But that didn't mean some of these people wouldn't be working for the government, developing dangerous weapons anyway. She looked back up at Luke impatiently. "I don't understand. What am I supposed to be looking for?"

He nodded and pointed at the pages. "Keep reading. Look for the one I circled."

Meg scanned each page and flipped to the next. Finally she found one entry, ringed in a neat ballpoint-pen circle. Meg read the words inside the circle, and felt herself become woozy. Suddenly, nothing made sense anymore, not Luke, not Drew, not the science center.

She looked up at Luke, utterly lost and more than a little angry. "What's the matter with you?" she spat at Luke, tears filling her eyes no matter how hard she tried not to let it happen. "Are you *trying* to break up Drew and me?"

Luke paused a long moment, looking a little stunned at her outburst. He adjusted his glasses and spoke very quietly. "You know what I always liked about you, Meg? That you always liked to look deeper into things, to not just take them at face value."

"What's your point, Luke?" Meg demanded.

"My point is, since you met Drew, all you've been doing is taking things at face value."

"I have not!"

Now Luke's voice rose as well. "You have too! You take everything Drew says as gospel!"

"Drew happens to be very smart!"

"I'm sure he is," Luke replied, rolling his eyes. "But you need to make up your own mind, Meg, about everything, and not just blindly accept everything everyone tells you! I bet you don't even think of this housing issue as *a* cause, but as *Drew's* cause!" He pointed to the circled entry on the papers Meg was holding. "Things aren't always black and white, even if someone as smart as Drew tells you they are!"

Meg reeled from Luke's words, as well as from what was written on the pages he'd given her. She didn't know how to respond to any of it. So, instead, she merely walked to the door of the store, as though she were in a trance.

"Meg," Luke called out to her.

Meg couldn't look back at him, just put her hand on the doorknob and waited.

"Are you still going to go to Drew's rally tomorrow?"

Meg thought about it for a long time. "I'm not sure," she finally answered.

Luke nodded, looking down at the floor tiles.

"Are you ever planning on coming back in here?"

Meg thought about her answer to that question even longer. When she finally spoke, it wasn't much more than a whisper. "I'm not sure." She walked out the door into the cold afternoon. It might have been a good day for the Irish, but it had been a terrible day for Meg Pryor.

Nine

Church on Sunday morning had been nearly unbearable. What Meg had needed was activity, something to keep her mind off what had happened the day before: the meeting in Drew's dorm room, her conversation with Luke, and the papers Luke had shown her. Meg still had them with her, folded into her small purse, and had even gone to the bathroom during church to look at them for the fiftieth time, still needing to make sure what she read was actually there. It was.

Meg needed to keep busy, to dance or shop or even do homework, anything to keep her mind occupied. Instead, she'd spent the morning crammed in the middle of a pew between Patty and an exceptionally squirmy Will. When Father Ryan had told them all to pray silently for a moment toward the end of the service, it was all Meg could do to keep from screaming.

The drive home had been even worse. Will and Patty were abuzz discussing the movie the family was going to see, which made Meg feel like dirt. Not only had Drew and Luke turned her life upside down yesterday, now Meg had to watch her family go off and have a wonderful time without her. And how was she going to be spending the afternoon? With a boy who might or might not even realize she was even there.

Meg's mother turned the family car into the driveway, and Meg's dad came out of the garage, wiping his hands on a rag. Meg could see he'd been painting a chair leg—he was forever halfway through some project in his garage workshop—and she hoped he hadn't noticed that any paint had been put back in an improper place.

But Jack Pryor only beamed, and opened the car's back door so Will and Patty could step out. "Hey, there they are, fans of Hollywood entertainment," he said.

"Did JJ call?" Will asked urgently.

"Not yet," Jack told him. "We'll probably hear from him after we get home."

Will's face turned disappointed. "Oh," he said. Then, as he switched gears, his face lit up again. "I'm ready to go," Will said excitedly. "I'm ready to go right now!"

His father grinned. "Take it easy, Thrill. The

movie doesn't start until five o'clock."

"What movie are we seeing?" Patty wanted to know.

"*My Fair Lady*," her father told her.

Will frowned. "It doesn't sound like there are any Martians in that. Or doctors from outer space."

"No, but I bet you'll like it anyway. You'll at least like the popcorn," Jack pointed out.

Will's face brightened. "Yeah!"

"I thought we'd all get cleaned up and go out for a late lunch, then ice cream, then hit the theater," Jack offered.

Patty looked at her father as if he had lost his mind. "Who ever heard of getting cleaned up after a hard day at church?"

Jack jokingly menaced her with his paint-covered fingers. "Well, *I* need to clean up, at least. Is that all right with you?"

Patty only rolled her eyes and walked past him into the house with Will. Jack rolled his eyes in imitation, drawing a laugh from his wife. "I used to be able to make Patty laugh," he said. "Now sometimes I wonder if she'll ever laugh again."

Helen patted his arm. "She's just at that age."

Jack nodded and turned to Meg, who was getting out of the car. Any lightness in his expression faded from his face. "Meg," he said simply.

"Dad," she replied.

"I'd say we'd bring you back something from Dairy Queen, but I don't even know if you like Dairy Queen anymore."

Meg knew that wasn't true. Her father knew full well that she loved Dairy Queen ice cream. "Thanks anyway," she said, instead of challenging his comment. "But if you take it into the movie with you, it'd only melt before I got it anyway."

"I guess so," her father nodded. "Do you have any idea what time you'll be home tonight?"

"Not late," Meg answered.

"Good," her dad said. "We'll tell you all about our afternoon as soon as we see you, then."

"Can't wait," Meg replied tightly.

Suddenly, Roxanne came running up, out of breath and looking determined. "Meg, come on, we have to go!"

"Where are we going?" Meg wanted to know.

"Yeah, Meg doesn't have a lot of time, Roxanne," Meg's dad explained helpfully. "Meg has big plans for the afternoon."

Meg glared at her father, and turned back to Roxanne, who was tugging her arm, pulling her toward the street. "I have some time, still. Let's go. You can tell me on the way."

As Meg set off with Roxanne, she took one last look back at her father, who was watching her go, standing still in the driveway.

"I wish I could have changed clothes," Meg said as they hurried along. "Now I'm going to be wearing my church clothes all day!"

"Who *cares* what you're wearing?" Roxanne grumbled impatiently. "This is much more important than that!"

Meg knew Roxanne was seriously upset. Otherwise, she'd never say something as crazy as, "Who *cares* what you're wearing?"

A city bus pulled to a stop across the street from them. Roxanne pulled Meg into the street. "Come on, that's our bus," she cried. Unfortunately they hadn't crossed at an intersection or a crosswalk, and several cars screeched to angry halts as the girls dashed across the road. Meg would have seen her life flash before her eyes, but there simply wasn't enough time. However, she did get a good scare out of it.

"Gosh, Rox," Meg gasped as they clambered onto the bus, the door hissing closed behind them. "If you're going to get us killed, could you at least tell me why?"

Rox sat down in a seat just behind the bus driver and Meg sat next to her. Roxanne leaned forward and looked out the windshield. "Excuse me," she called to the driver. "Can't you go any faster? I have to get to my boyfriend's as soon as possible!"

The bus driver, an older man, turned around and looked balefully at her from beneath his cap. "I don't care if you're late for a date with Chuck Bednarik," he said slowly. "This bus goes where it goes, as fast as it goes, so sit back and enjoy the ride."

Roxanne sat back, but she didn't look particularly relaxed. "Who's Chuck Bednarik?" she asked Meg.

"He used to play for the Eagles," Meg answered, and when Roxanne gave her a surprised look, Meg added, "He was a big star football player. JJ talked about him all the time." But Meg had other matters on her mind. "This is the bus to Lenny's place," she said in sudden realization.

Roxanne leaned forward and looked out the front of the bus again, as though perhaps it had magically teleported itself closer to her eventual destination. "I've decided to follow your advice," she told Meg. "If I'm going to lose Lenny to that . . . *new girl,* I'm not going to go quietly!"

"What do you mean?" Meg asked, and even as she asked it, she was glad for a split second that she was with Roxanne. Even though her best friend was in crisis, dealing with it was much better than sitting around the house worrying more about Luke and Drew.

"I'm going to catch him in the act with that Sherry," Roxanne explained. "I'm going to force him to tell me the truth, and then I'll just walk away, and he'll know exactly what he's missing!"

"Wow," Meg said, impressed with the plan and Rox's newfound determination. Then she frowned. "Wait, what do you need *me* for?"

Rox looked at Meg as though the answer was obvious. "Moral support."

Meg nodded. "Oh," she said. "As long as that's all you need. I'm not dressed for anything else."

The bus groaned to a stop, and the girls dashed to the door. The bus driver paused teasingly before cranking the handle that would let Meg and Roxanne out. "Tell Chuck I said hi," he said. "Tell him it ain't been the same since he retired."

"I can't tell anyone anything if you don't open

the stupid doors!" Rox shouted in frustration. The driver smiled and pulled the handle.

The girls stepped onto the curb and the bus pulled away from them, leaving a cloud of smelly exhaust behind. Meg and Rox quickly covered the remaining distance to Lenny's grandmother's apartment building. Once there, Roxanne started around to the rear of the building. "Wait, what are you doing?" Meg asked.

"We're going up the fire escape in the back," Rox explained quickly. "We have to surprise Lenny, remember?"

Meg looked down at her dress shoes, which were not made for climbing rickety fire escapes, then back at the building's stoop. "Can't we surprise him by going in the front door?"

Roxanne put her hands on her hips as though the answer was obvious. "What, we're supposed to ring the doorbell and let him answer it? How is that surprising anyone?"

Meg couldn't think of a reply to that, so she followed Rox into the trash-strewn alley and around the corner to the back of the building. The two girls ducked under laundry lines and stepped between garbage cans to the iron fire escape. Meg looked up uncertainly.

But Roxanne had already dragged a garbage can beneath the ladder and was climbing atop it. Luckily, there was enough garbage in it that the can was heavy enough to support her weight. "You'll be fine," she said, and leaped up to grab the lowest rung of the ladder. Her feet kicked out as she pulled herself up and climbed through the floor of the fire escape's first level.

"Very ladylike," Meg commented dryly.

"Who cares about ladylike," Rox retorted. "This is a matter of life and death! Come on!"

Not wanting to be left behind, Meg climbed onto the trash can. The slick soles of her dress shoes slid against the aluminum of the can, and she nearly fell off. But she caught her balance, thinking, *Thank goodness for all that dancing!* took a deep breath and leaped for the ladder, her hands finding the cold metal rung. As she reached for the next rung up, Meg felt one of her shoes start to slide from her foot, and she had to point her toe to keep it on. Finally she managed to get far enough up the ladder that she could place her feet on a rung and step back into her shoe. "Hurry up," Roxanne called from above, and a moment later, Meg joined her on the first landing.

Meg followed Rox up the stairs. Turning the

corner to the second landing, they came upon an old woman leaning out her open window and smoking. She looked startled to see them, and coughed on her cigarette smoke. "Burglars!" she shouted in a heavy accent. Then she paused, looked at them a little closer, and went right back to screaming. "Very young, pretty burglars! Help! Help!"

"Shh! Shh!" Roxanne urged frantically. "We're not burglars!"

The old woman squinted at them suspiciously. "No? I was going to say, you're dressed very nicely for burglars, I think."

"That's right," Meg jumped in helpfully. "We're dressed this way because we're here for a surprise birthday party. For my friend's grandmother."

"Your grandmother," the old woman repeated. "Who is she? I know everybody in this building."

Roxanne and Meg paused, on the spot, having to think of a name. But then the woman scratched her chin and added, "Except the lady who moved in two weeks ago."

"That's her," Roxanne said quickly, then stumbled through an improvised name. "Esther Grana . . . masov . . . ski."

"Esther Granamasovski," the old woman repeated.

Meg decided the woman must repeat everything she heard. "Why wasn't I invited?"

"Her grandmother's very shy," Meg answered.

Roxanne nodded vigorously. "That's right. She hates parties, and insists we keep them very small, even if they're total surprises to her."

"Total surprise," the old woman said, nodding. "I suppose I can go up tomorrow and introduce myself, after all the excitement."

"She'd love that," Roxanne said.

"Maybe I'll even bring some of my famous banana bread, or a nice *kugel*. Does your grandmother like peach *kugel*?"

Roxanne didn't even know what it was. But that didn't stop her. "She sure does. It's her favorite."

"Then I've got a full day ahead of me in the kitchen," the old woman said with a grin, waving good-bye. She ducked back into her apartment, closing the window after her. The girls looked at each other for a moment, and Meg burst into giggles, unable to help herself. "Oh my God," she said through her laughter. "Esther Granamasovski?"

Roxanne turned to the next set of steps on the fire escape. "It was the best I could come up with on short notice," she said.

"At least someone's going to wind up with

banana bread and peach . . . thingie," Meg said with a grin.

The two girls continued up the fire escape. On the next level, they passed a window that was closed, but the curtains were open, and inside Meg could see an older couple. He was watching a wrestling match on television, and she was painting a large canvas by numbers, filling in sections of an outline of a landscape with different colors.

Looking in the window, Meg was reminded of a movie her mother had once told her about. The movie was called *Rear Window,* and it was about a photographer who had a broken leg. All the photographer could do all day was sit and stare out his window and into the windows of his neighbors. He became convinced that one of his neighbors had committed a murder, and set out to prove it. Meg had never seen the film, but it sounded exciting, dangerous, and a little scary—*Kind of like,* she thought, *climbing up a fire escape in dress shoes.* Meg remembered that both Luke and Drew liked the man who made the movie, a director named Alfred Hitchcock.

Meg angrily shook her head, dispelling the thought. She didn't want to be thinking about Luke and Drew right now. Meg decided to think of this adventure as more like an episode of *The Man from U.N.C.L.E.*, a new television spy show she enjoyed very much.

On the next landing, Meg found Roxanne standing very still, looking at a black cat that was sitting on the metal grating before her. Its back arched as it hissed angrily. "It's just a cat," Meg said, puzzled. "Keep going!"

"I can't," Rox replied fearfully. "It's a *black* cat! If I cross its path, it's bad luck!"

"I think that's only if the cat crosses *your* path, Rox."

"What's the difference?" Roxanne wanted to know. "If I cross it, does it matter?"

Meg didn't have the slightest idea. But she wanted to get off this fire escape sometime before the end of the century. "If you cross it, nothing bad will happen. In fact, you'll have *good* luck."

Roxanne squinted at her suspiciously. "Are you making that up?"

"No," Meg assured her friend. "Patty told me she read it in a book of ancient superstitions."

Roxanne stepped gingerly around the cat, who kept its back arched, watching them warily. "Well, if Patty read it, it's good enough for me," Roxanne said.

They left the cat behind, and at last came to the fifth floor. Rox gestured at one of the windows facing them. "That should be Lenny's grandmother's bedroom," she said. Then she paused, just looking at the window.

"What's the matter?" Meg asked. "Open it up!"

"It's weird," Roxanne said slowly. "Now that I'm here, part of me doesn't want to know. You know?"

"You've come this far, Roxanne," Meg pointed out. "I think you have to know at this point!"

Roxanne twirled her brown hair around her finger. "I suppose you're right."

She bent down and carefully pulled at the edge of the window. It slid smoothly and quietly up an inch. Roxanne kept pulling, trying hard not to make any sound at all. When the window was open enough to accommodate them, Rox slipped inside, and Meg followed.

As she pulled her back leg into Lenny's grandmother's bedroom, Meg lost her balance and lurched sideways into a floor lamp. Her heart jumped in her chest. The lamp was just about to crash to the floor when she kicked out her leg and caught it atop her ankle, inches off the ground.

No sound had been made. Roxanne put an anguished finger to her lips and glared at Meg. *Shhh!*

Meg smiled apologetically and placed the lamp back upright. As she did, both girls heard a voice from another room. "Just like that." It was Lenny. And he was talking to someone.

Meg looked at Roxanne, who stood frozen in the bedroom, midway between the frilly bed and an antique armoire. Yellowed photographs of ancient relatives grimaced at them from the walls. "Like this?" they heard a voice reply. Sherry. Roxanne's hands balled into fists at the sound of her voice.

"Perfect," Lenny said. "That's really great. Now, take your time . . ."

Roxanne turned to look at Meg, tears in her eyes. Meg's mouth was open in a shocked gasp at what they'd heard. How could Lenny? After all the things he'd said to Roxanne, after all the time they'd spent together . . . How could he?!

Roxanne stormed out of the bedroom and into the hall, Meg hot on her heels. "Lenny Beeber," Roxanne was shouting, "you good-for-nothing, slimy, cheating, two-timing, backstabbing sack of—"

The girls stomped around the corner into the living room of the apartment, and pulled up short. In front of them, on the couch, sat Lenny and Sherry. But they weren't fooling around, as Meg and Roxanne had assumed. No, Sherry was holding

Lenny's bass, and Lenny sitting next to her, demonstrating where Sherry should place her fingers on the frets.

"Um," Roxanne managed to say, her face blank.

"Hi, baby," Lenny said, smiling. "Decided to sneak in and surprise me, huh? Hi, Meg."

"She was . . . that is, we were . . . ," Meg tried to explain. "Um," she finished.

"I thought you were . . . ," Rox started again.

"This is Sherry," Lenny said, gesturing to the pretty girl beside him. "I decided to start giving bass lessons, and she's my first student."

"I think we've already met," Sherry said to the girls. "Hello again."

Roxanne blinked several times, perhaps hoping doing so would make the situation easier to understand. "Bass lessons?"

Lenny rose from the couch and crossed to stand in front of Roxanne, smiling down at her. "See, I happen to know that a certain best girlfriend in the world is having a birthday soon, so I figured I'd earn a little extra money so I could buy an extra special present."

Meg looked from Lenny to Sherry and back. She couldn't believe any of this. How could they have been so wrong?

"I've wanted to learn how to play bass for a long

time," Sherry said. "I broke up with my last boyfriend because he wouldn't teach me how to play. He was a bass player. I think he felt threatened. But my new boyfriend, Steve, doesn't mind at all. He doesn't play any instruments."

"Your . . . *new* boyfriend . . . Steve?" Roxanne started to cry again, this time out of embarrassment. "I can't believe this. I can't believe it! I'm so stupid!"

Lenny laughed and put his arms around her. "You thought I was cheating on you? I think that's sweet, that you'd get so jealous and go to all this trouble."

Roxanne sniffled and looked up at him. "You do?"

"Definitely. And you just keep on doing what you're doing—checking things out for yourself to get to the truth. But next time, you could just ask me."

Now Roxanne had to laugh. Meg, meanwhile, was reminded by Lenny's words about "checking things out for yourself" of her conversation with Luke the day before, and of her impending encounter with Drew. She glanced at her watch and saw it was much later than she thought. "Oh no," she muttered. "I have to hurry up and get to Penn!"

"I could give you a ride," Sherry volunteered,

turning to smile at Lenny and Roxanne. "It looks like my lesson is over, anyway."

Meg beamed. "Could you? That'd be great!"

Lenny gestured to the front door. "Meg, it might be easier for you to go out that way than the way you came in."

Meg smiled sheepishly and headed to the door with Sherry. "Hey, Meg," Roxanne called out to her. "Thanks for sticking by me. I knew I could count on you."

Meg smiled brightly. "I'm glad everything worked out okay. I guess that black cat was good luck after all, huh?"

Roxanne smiled back. Meg and Sherry stepped out of the apartment, and hurried down the stairs to Sherry's car.

Ten

"**R**oxanne seems really terrific," Sherry said as her new Ford zipped through the Philadelphia streets toward the Penn campus. "Have you been friends for a long time?"

"A very long time," Meg replied. Her thoughts were several miles ahead, already with Drew, wondering how she was going to face him, what he would say when he saw what was written on the papers Luke had given her.

"She's a great girlfriend, too. She and Lenny are so good together. He talks about her all the time."

Meg turned to Sherry, feeling a little sheepish. "I'm sorry about busting in on you back there. That wasn't very nice of us."

Sherry waved Meg off, smiling. "Don't worry about it. I would have done the same thing in her situation, probably."

"You would have?"

Sherry nodded. "Especially with my old boyfriend. He was my first, you know. And when

146

you're really in love for the first time, you can be a little crazy. Always thinking about him, always worrying about things you've said, always making up the worst possible situations in your mind. Sometimes it can blind you to the bigger picture."

Meg looked out the window. That was a pretty accurate description of her feelings about Drew. Did that mean she was in love with him?

"You must have a boyfriend," Sherry wanted to know. "Right?"

Meg chewed on a thumbnail. "Yes," she replied, then changed her mind. "No. I don't know."

Sherry smiled. "If you don't know, then you don't. Sorry, but when it's right and you both feel it, that's when you know."

Meg felt her stomach drop. It just got worse and worse. Now a complete stranger was telling her that things weren't going to work out with Drew.

Sherry seemed to sense Meg's discouragement, and smiled hopefully. "But hey, I don't believe in love at first sight. Sometimes one person realizes it before the other, and it takes a little while for the other person to come around," she said. "That's what happened with Steve and me."

Meg nodded. That *was* helpful news, if it was true.

Sherry looked at Meg for a long moment. "You don't go to Penn."

Meg shook her head.

Sherry nodded. "So you're going there right now to see your . . . not-yet-boyfriend."

"That's right."

"And today might be the day you find out if he's ever going to lose the 'not-yet' tag."

Meg sighed. "Maybe."

Sherry nodded sympathetically. "I hope it works out."

Meg looked out the window once more. "Me too," she said.

A few minutes later, Sherry pulled her car to a stop in front of Drew's dorm. Meg closed the car door behind her and leaned down to look in the window. "Thanks," she said.

Sherry gave a little wave. "No problem. Good luck. When I see you at *Bandstand,* you can tell me how it all turned out." She pulled her car back into traffic, leaving Meg at the curb.

Meg hurried up the steps and into the building. She had a suspicion she was late and had already missed Drew, Cliff, Dan, Greg, and Natalie, but she wanted to check, just to be sure. On her way up the stairs, she found Beth coming out of the bathroom. "Meg," Beth said, surprised. "What are you doing here? Did I forget to give you something for JJ's care package?"

"No," Meg said, glancing at her watch. "I'm actually here to see Drew. He and I . . . we were going to . . . we had plans."

"Oh, well, Drew left a little while ago," Beth told her. "With a bunch of other people."

Meg turned and hurried back down the stairs, leaving her brother's bewildered fiancée behind. "Okay, thanks," she called back. "I'll talk to you later!"

Meg crossed the boundary of the campus and into the depressed neighborhood where she, Drew, and the others had confronted the assessors the weekend before. Meg muttered silent curses to herself with every step. Now Drew might be angry with her, might think she had decided not to come at all, or maybe would think that she didn't take important issues seriously. Maybe he had even left her signs behind in his room. She definitely did not have a good feeling about her upcoming encounter with Drew.

Not that she even knew exactly where to find

him. He could be anywhere in this neighborhood. Fortunately, she didn't have to walk far before she heard a commotion, with lots of voices involved.

Meg rounded a corner, following the sounds, and pulled up short. A crowd of people, black and white, had gathered around a tenement stoop. On the stoop, Drew, Dan, Greg, Natalie, Cliff, and several other students stood side-by-side, their arms linked so they blocked the building's entry from the team of assessors standing impatiently in front of them. Meg's signs leaned against the stone facing of the stoop, forgotten for the moment. *At least Drew remembered to bring them,* Meg thought.

Everyone seemed to be talking at once. Cliff was shouting, red-faced, at one of the assessors. The assessor was shouting back. Drew, Dan, Greg, and Natalie were speaking less loudly, but just as urgently, with other members of the assessor team. Neighborhood residents yelled at nobody in particular, just urging on the general commotion. And more people were coming out of nearby buildings or walking over from other streets to join in.

To Meg, the air felt heavy with trouble, the way it had surrounding her father's store on the day of the riots. These people were ready to fight. Meg wondered for a moment if there were going to be fights everywhere she went for the rest of her life.

"Back off this stoop right now, because there's no way you're getting through me," Cliff roared at the lead assessor. A restless murmur worked its way through the crowd.

"You young punk," the assessor snarled back. "I don't know who gave you the right to talk back to your elders, but—"

"Elder doesn't mean better or smarter," Cliff fired back.

"But it does mean someone who can wipe up the floor with you, if you don't let us do our job," the man growled, and charged at Cliff. Cliff braced himself, ready for the fight to start, but the assessor's colleagues grabbed their associate and held him back.

Drew stepped forward, breaking the arm-to-arm link with Dan and Natalie, and put a hand on Cliff's shoulder. "Cliff, that's enough! Look around you! We've gotten this neighborhood's people to stand up for themselves. Let them take it from here!"

Cliff yanked free of Drew and returned to taunting the assessor. "You think you can just waltz in anywhere you want and force people with less dough than you, with less opportunity than you, to pack up and move out just 'cause you say so?"

Drew shook his head in exasperation, looking around the steadily worsening scene. Finally, his eyes fell on Meg, standing at the back of the crowd, worried lines creasing her pretty face. Meg waved uncertainly. There was no way he could reach her.

Meg took a deep breath and plunged into the crowd, working her way toward the stoop. She vanished into a sea of overcoats, a cloud of leather and aftershave and sweat, and thought she might actually drown. Jostled from side to side, she nearly lost her balance several times. "Excuse me, excuse me," she gasped. But she didn't think anybody heard her.

Meg forced herself through the tight spaces between bodies, only hoping she was going in the right direction. Where once she thought she knew exactly why she was doing what she was doing, now she was less certain than ever.

Finally, just when Meg was sure she wouldn't be able to draw another breath, she found herself at the first step of the building's stoop. Hair mussed, church clothes rumpled and askew, she pushed her way from one step to the next, angling to the side of the stoop, her hip finally pressed painfully into the low stone facing.

Above her, she caught a glimpse of Drew in the sea of bodies. "Drew!" she yelled.

"Let her through," she heard Drew yell to the crowd massed into the tight space. "Let her through!"

Meg struggled up another step, then another. She was perhaps two steps away from the top of the stoop when someone shoved into her from the side, perhaps shoved by someone else in turn. It didn't matter. All Meg knew was that she had lost her balance, and was tipping sideways, over the stone facing.

Time slowed to a crawl. Meg had a moment to look down below her, over the side of the steps. It wasn't a long way to the ground, but there was no way she was going to land on her feet. This was going to hurt. A lot.

As her body tilted sideways, almost parallel to the ground, Meg managed to look back and catch another glimpse of Drew's face. He could see what was happening, and his expression was one of terror as he tried to push toward her. But he was still so far away!

And then Meg's perspective went crazy, twirling and spinning, everything turning upside down as she plunged over the stone facing. The hard ground rushed up at her, her hands flailed out below and above her, and Meg braced herself as best she could for the pain she knew was about to come—

Suddenly Meg stopped moving with a jerk. Something had caught her left hand, sending a bolt of pain into her shoulder before strong arms pulled her back, setting her upright in a sitting position on the wall. Meg gasped for breath, turning her head. It was Drew! Somehow, he had crossed the distance and caught her at the last possible moment. He took her face in his hands and looked into her eyes. "Meg! Are you okay?" he shouted.

Meg nodded, still in shock. Her whole body shuddered.

Drew looked back over his shoulder. There was more pushing and shoving between the students and the assessors. Dan was having no luck holding Cliff back. "Let's get you out of here for a second," Drew said.

He hopped nimbly over the wall and down to the ground, landing gracefully. He held his arms up for Meg, and she slid down into them. Drew lowered her to the ground, took her hand, and walked her a distance away from the tumult in front of the building.

"Are you sure you're okay?" he wanted to know,

now that the space around them was a little calmer.

"I'm fine," she assured him, her shakes finally starting to vanish. "Just a little scared."

He nodded in relief, then managed a small smile. "I didn't think you were coming," he said.

"I'm sorry I was late," Meg replied. "I got . . . I had to help Roxanne with something."

Drew grabbed her hand, and Meg felt that familiar bolt of happy electricity run up her arm and down her back, making her tingle—a different kind of shiver. "I have to go back up there," he said apologetically. "If we don't get this under control soon, Cliff's going to ruin any chance we have of being taken seriously. That's if someone hasn't called the cops on us already."

Meg nodded, understanding.

He looked at her seriously. "I'll understand if you don't want to come with me, not after what just . . ."

Meg tugged away from Drew, hating to do it. "Drew, I can't go up there with you, but that's not why."

"Why not?" Drew asked, his eyes narrowing.

Meg looked for a long moment into those eyes. This was the moment of truth. She could easily say "forget it," change her mind, and go up there on that stoop with Drew, pretending the past few days hadn't happened at all. She could try to forget everything Luke had said to her, and try to forget her own feelings of conflict and uncertainty.

But she knew she couldn't do any of those things. Because, she knew, once you know something and it makes you feel a certain way, you can never un-know or un-feel. Trying to do either wouldn't be right, and it wouldn't be honest—to Drew, or herself. And she didn't want to be with Drew if it meant she couldn't be honest.

So, instead of saying "forget it," Meg took a deep breath, held it, opened her purse, and pulled out the pieces of paper Luke had given her. She carefully unfolded them and handed them to Drew. "It's a list of possible tenants for the science center," she explained.

Drew took the list, and looked it over curiously. Meg watched his eyes, and knew the moment he got to the entry that Luke had circled. He looked up, and Meg nodded. "A juvenile polio research facility," she said.

"Your little brother," Drew replied.

Meg nodded again. "I can't be one hundred percent opposed to the science center when it might include something that could help kids like Will. Even if it just makes them less scared, or helps them understand a little better. Even that would be a good thing.

"Will's going to have surgery soon," she went on, "and he doesn't know exactly what for, or what could happen, because no one will tell him. Maybe nobody knows. But a research facility might help everyone get the answers they want, and I can't be against that."

Meg couldn't tell if Drew was disappointed or not. He looked at her neutrally, his eyes betraying no emotion. "No," he said. "I guess you can't."

Meg put a hand on his chest, trying to reassure him. "I haven't made up my mind one way or the other about the science center and all the issues about moving people out of their homes and all that stuff," she said. "I just want some more time to think about all sides of the issue, and then decide . . . for myself."

Drew took her hand, and looked earnestly into her eyes. "Meg, you're right, there are a lot of sides to this issue," he said. "And what's going on with your brother is an important one. But what's also important is the voice of the students! This is an important event for us, one that could determine how successfully we can protest other things for years to come! I thought that mattered to you!"

Meg looked up at the building and saw black families leaning out their windows and looking down at the increasingly intense rally below them. They looked concerned, confused, and a little bit frightened. "I think what you're doing is good, and it should be done," Meg told Drew, then pointed to the families. "I think they think so, too. But did you talk about it with them? Did you ask the people who actually live here how they wanted to handle this? Because they might have said they wanted to do it in a way other than having a street fight on their doorstep."

Drew looked at the windows, the expression on his face slowly changing. "This isn't just about the student voice, and that's all you've been talking about this entire time," Meg reminded him gently. "This isn't just about my little brother, either. It's about a lot of things, and when dealing with an issue this important, don't you have to think about all of those things?"

Drew finally looked back at Meg, and smiled tenderly and apologetically. "You're right," he said at last, then laughed a little. "I guess it doesn't matter how good my grades are. I can still be pretty stupid."

Meg shook her head. "You're not stupid. You

care about things, important things, and so many people don't. It's not always easy to do the right things or the hard things—that's what my dad always says. But you're trying. I think that makes you wonderful."

Drew shook his head. "I think *you're* wonderful."

Meg blinked, unsure of what she'd just heard. "You do?"

Drew nodded, pulling Meg close and kissing her deeply. "Thank you for reminding me what I already knew—that you're so much more than a pretty face."

Meg kept her eyes closed after the kiss, so swept away was she in the moment. Of all the ways she thought this conversation might end up, she hadn't allowed herself to hope it might be this way. At last she opened her eyes, and smiled up at Drew, who was smiling back. He jerked a thumb back over his shoulder. "I better call this off so we can go home and think of the most effective way to protest—that looks at all sides."

They turned to face the building stoop. Cliff, battling against Dan's efforts to restrain him, pulled free and shoved the assessor, who shoved back. Punches broke out on the stoop, the crowd volume increasing as shouts filled the air. Drew frowned.

"And it looks like I better call this off right now."

Before he could even take a step toward the stoop, four police cars screeched onto the street, lights flashing. They parked at the curb, and officers got out, nightsticks in hand. Meg recognized the policeman with the droopy eyes—her uncle's friend, Buddy Kelley. Meg raised a hand to shield her face from the policeman. "I better go, too," she said to Drew. She started away.

But Drew pulled her back. "Not just yet," he said. And he tilted his head and gave her another kiss, this one even deeper than the one before. In the midst of it, Meg had time to think, *Maybe Roxanne's black cat was good luck for me, too.* It was amazing how few things worked out the way you expected them to, especially if you spent hours and hours thinking about how you expected them to happen.

Drew ended the kiss, placing his forehead against hers. "I'll see you later?" he asked.

"Count on it," Meg whispered back. And she walked away, holding his hand to the very last possible moment.

Meg was still smiling as she heard the sounds of the protest diminish behind her. The air didn't seem quite as cold as it had before, her steps not as heavy.

Drew understood her position, she felt better for having made a decision of her own, and she no longer had to keep any secrets from her family.

Suddenly, Meg stopped on the street that bordered the university and the depressed neighborhood. She had forgotten. There was still one very important piece of business she had left to take care of, and ultimately, it might be the most important piece of business of all.

Eleven

Sunday afternoon was never the busiest time at Vinyl Crocodile, and today was no exception. Sunday, Meg thought, was a day for families to sit around the television watching football, or to stand in the kitchen making the weekend's big dinner feast. Of course, for some, it was a day to protest social injustice. The one thing Sunday wasn't, usually, was a day to buy records.

Consequently, Sunday was Luke's favorite day to work. The store's owner would have preferred to close the shop, but Luke had persuaded him to leave it open. "You never know when someone might straggle in," Luke told him. "And I don't mind being here and I could get a lot of your paperwork done."

In truth, there really wasn't much paperwork to do; Luke was able to get through it pretty easily the day before. So Sunday was sort of a "day off at work" for Luke. Having the whole place to himself, he'd put some of his favorite music on the store's stereo—Woody Guthrie's folk songs, or perhaps something jazzy, like John Coltrane or Thelonious Monk—and then he'd sit behind the counter and reread favorite sections of Jack Kerouac's *Dharma Bums*. Occasionally, Sam would come by, sit in the listening booth for an hour or two, and maybe chat with Luke a little bit. But for the most part, the store was deserted all day.

It was deserted when Meg walked in. The bell over the door chimed softly, barely audible over the cool groan of Miles Davis's trumpet over the store hi-fi. Meg could see Luke leaning back in his chair behind the counter, his tattered paperback copy of Kerouac's book spread open facedown before him. He was staring into the space at the back of the store. He hadn't heard her come in.

From this angle, Meg thought, Luke looked very handsome. He looked like he was thinking about great things, important things, and Meg could envision him as a teacher someday, or maybe even a president.

"Hello," she said quietly.

Luke didn't move. Whatever he was thinking about, he was thinking about it very deeply.

Meg crossed the checkered floor to the counter, her good shoes making a *clack-clack* sound in unconscious rhythm to the trumpet music. Finally she stood across the counter from Luke, and rested her hands lightly on it. "Hello," she said again.

Luke jumped, startled, as though he'd been suddenly awakened from a dream. In fact, he jumped so much that he fell out of the chair and crashed to the floor. Meg couldn't help but giggle, the seriousness of the conversation she intended to have momentarily forgotten. *Very unpresidential,* she thought, and giggled all over again. "Oh, Luke," she said between bursts of laughter, "I'm so sorry!"

Luke got up, grumpy, and rubbed his sore rear end. "Is this what you're doing for fun these days? Sneaking up on people?"

"Sneaking up?" Meg yelped, incredulous. "Sneaking up?! It's not like I climbed in your back window through a fire escape or something!"

Luke lifted his chair upright once more, and looked at her like she was crazy. "We're on the first floor," he pointed out. "We don't have a fire escape. What are you talking about?"

"Uh, never mind," Meg said quickly. "I didn't sneak up on you. I came right in through the front door. I even said hello, but you were, I don't know, thinking about Bob Dylan's real name!"

"His real name is Bob Zimmerman," Luke told

her, then looked away. "And that wasn't what I was thinking about. Aren't you supposed to be at your rally?"

"It ended before it started, actually," Meg replied. "I wasn't going to stay for it anyway, and you knew that, didn't you?"

Luke wouldn't look at her, and Meg knew she was right. She took the papers out of her purse and set them on the counter, turning them around to face him.

"Luke, why did you show me this research on the science center?"

He didn't look at the papers. He picked up his book, then put it down again. Then he closed it, and put it on the shelf under the counter.

Meg tried again. "I'm serious, Luke. I really want to understand. I thought you were against the science center!"

"I am," he answered. "That hasn't changed. But I knew the stuff I found in that research might change *your* mind, and . . . and there's room for more than one opinion in the world, you know? For instance, some people like Bob Dylan, and some people don't.

"And I don't like those people, but that's just me," he added. "They still have a right to make up their own minds."

Meg wasn't sure she understood. "But why tell me about it? That's the part I don't get." She took a deep breath, then asked the real question. "Luke, I want you to answer me for real this time: Are you trying to break up Drew and me?"

Now Luke looked at her, his eyes boring into her, as they hadn't since . . . since . . . Meg couldn't remember the last time he'd looked at her that way. Was it back when they were dating? "No. That's the last thing I want to do."

"Then why . . . ?"

"I told you about it because I owe it to you to tell you things like this—as a *friend*. If you're involved in something that's important to you, then you need to know the full situation. And if I can help you do that—as a *friend*—then I should."

Meg nodded, feeling a bit silly. She had concocted all these crazy ideas that Luke was out to get her, when all he had been trying to do was be there for her. But something still nagged at her, and though she felt even sillier pressing on, she had to finish this. "Okay," she said. "Thanks. But Luke, I can't help but feel like that's not all that's been bothering you for the last couple days. Am I crazy, or is there something else that's been going on?"

Luke looked away again, suddenly fidgety, and

Meg knew she had hit on something important. Usually, you could ask Luke the most direct question, and he wouldn't even flinch. Meg had never seen Luke like this before.

"Well," he started slowly, "when we broke up . . ."

"Yes?" Meg replied, waiting for more.

"It was both our decisions. And it was a good thing to do. It was the right thing. I really, really believe that, Meg. And I'm glad we've stayed friends."

"Me too," Meg agreed.

"But . . . I don't know . . ." He looked like he was suddenly in pain, just saying the words. "That doesn't mean I like hearing about Drew all the time. About how great he is, and things like that."

Meg was dumbstruck. Of all the things she expected to hear, that wasn't it. "But I just asked you if you were trying to . . ."

"I'm *not* trying to break you and Drew up," Luke repeated. "I'm not jealous. At least, I don't think I am, not really. But . . . I don't know . . . you've moved on from our relationship a lot faster than I have, I guess. Not everyone moves as fast as you do."

"Luke, I'm so sorry," Meg said, and she was. She

felt terrible for not noticing what she was doing. Of course, she realized, if she had been in Luke's position, and he had met somebody new and was crazy about her, it would have driven Meg around the bend to be around him, even if she wasn't romantically interested in Luke anymore.

Luke shrugged, trying to minimize the pain he was feeling. "It's just not my favorite topic, that's all."

Silence fell over them, a little sad. Something had changed between them weeks ago, but only now was it becoming something real and solid, that could be defined. "I guess we both have to be a little more sensitive about how we talk to each other," Meg suggested.

Luke nodded, but didn't look happy about it.

"I don't want to," Meg went on. "One of the things I loved about us was that I felt like I could tell you anything, and you could tell me anything."

"I feel the same way," Luke said. "But I really think this is for the best, at least for right now."

Meg thought about it and, as much as she didn't like it, there was no way Luke was wrong about this. If they wanted to stay friends, on any level, they would have to learn to filter the conversations between them. It wouldn't be the same, but it would be something, at least.

"So we're okay?" she asked of him, hopefully.

"We're better than okay," he responded with a smile. "Can I count on you for New Release Day this week?"

Meg found herself smiling back. "Hey, some things you can always count on," she told him. "Anything good coming in?"

"The Turtles," he told her. "And Joan Baez, I think."

"The Turtles I like," she said. "Joan Baez . . ."

"I'll be playing her when you come in," Luke promised. "And you'll love her."

"We'll see," Meg said, grinning, as she walked to the door. She waved to Luke. "I'll see you then. And Luke? Thanks."

Luke waved back, and smiled.

With the rally over, and her difficult, but rewarding, conversation with Luke behind her, Meg found herself waiting for the bus headed for home with the rest of the afternoon spread out at her feet. No one would be in the house, she remembered; they'd all be at the movies. Rox was with Lenny, Beth was probably studying, and maybe JJ would call, but maybe he wouldn't.

Meg sighed. That was what she got for making

plans that fell through, she realized. But she had to admit, a lot of good things had come from the past few days. She had found a new level of communication with Luke, and seen Rox do the same with Lenny. In fact, Meg had made a lot of strides in terms of communication with all sorts of people— including Drew and her family.

Meg found herself wondering if a person could actually feel herself change and grow. Just because that person was changing and growing in some unexpected ways didn't mean it wasn't happening. Meg thought about it and decided it was probably happening all the time, and only if you were lucky would you be able to notice it once in a while.

Something small and white fell before her eyes, then another, then another. Meg looked up into the gray sky. The first snow of the season was starting to fall. It had never happened this early in the year that Meg could remember. Everything really was changing, and Meg felt a little sad for a moment. As much as she wanted to grow up as soon as possible, there were some things she didn't want to leave behind.

And so, just as the bus pulled up, Meg turned and headed in the other direction.

• • •

There was a long line in front of the De Lux Theater, and it took Meg a moment to spot her family. But there they were, halfway to the ticket booth. From where she stood, across the street, it looked like her father was doing his terrible Jimmy Cagney imitation, the one he always did when the Pryors went to the movies. Frequently, JJ would accompany their dad with an equally terrible imitation of Edward G. Robinson. But JJ, of course, was not around, so today Jack Pryor was a solo act. It didn't matter; the entire family was laughing at his silly antics, even Patty.

Meg's mom suddenly noticed a dribble of ice cream on Will's coat, and crouched down to wipe it off with a handkerchief. Jack turned to Patty and indicated a spot on her coat with his finger. When Patty looked down, fooled, her father tipped his finger up, tapping Patty on the tip of her nose. The four of them dissolved into laughter once more.

This, Meg thought. *This is what I don't want to leave behind. And I don't have to, no matter how old I get. Do I?*

She crossed the street, still wearing her church clothes. Snow was starting to stick to the concrete. By the time the movie was over, it would be a perfect blanket, solid white and beautiful. If it kept up, there might soon be a snowman in the Pryor yard.

"Look," Will shouted, pointing. "It's Meg!"

All of their faces lit up as Meg approached, including, Meg was happy to see, her father's. Meg's mother wrapped her in a huge hug, and Will tugged at her coat. "We got Dad to change his mind about taking us to see *Goldfinger,* but Mom wouldn't let him," he told her. "So we're still going to see *My Fair Lady.*"

"I still want to see *Dr. Strangelove,*" Patty muttered.

Meg looked up at her father. "Finished up a little early, did you?" he asked.

Meg nodded, and gently pulled away from her mother. "Dad, can I talk to you for a minute?"

Jack Pryor looked at his wife Helen, who nodded encouragingly. "Sure," he said to Meg, and the two of them stepped out of line, moving a short distance away. They both shifted their weight from foot to foot uncomfortably, neither quite sure who should start.

Meg took a deep breath and decided to jump in. "Dad," she began.

But he cut her off with a wave of his hand. "I know," he said. "You weren't going to be with Beth today." Meg looked away. Her father put a finger under her chin and tilted her face to look at him again. "Your mother pointed out to me that if I rode you about it, you'd never tell us anything anymore, and I don't want that." He stuffed his hands in his pockets, and looked away, down the street. "So I guess I laid the guilt on a little thick."

Meg shook her head. "Dad, it's okay."

"Look, I didn't want to be around your grandparents all the time when I was your age. I get that." He hunched his shoulders and breathed out, watching the thin puff of air curl into the falling snowflakes. "But that doesn't mean I don't worry about you when you're out. I'll *always* worry about you, you know?"

Meg nodded. "I know."

Her father looked at her seriously. "And it doesn't mean that I don't want you around or that I don't want to spend time with you. Just know that, all right?"

Meg nodded again. "I know that, Dad."

Jack Pryor smiled, and put his arm around Meg, walking her back to the ticket line, where Helen, Patty, and Will had reached the front. "And try not to eat all of my popcorn this time, will you?"

Meg smiled gratefully at him, took the ticket Patty handed to her, and walked with her family into the theater.

The American Dreams "Dreams Come True" Sweepstakes
Official Rules

NO PURCHASE NECESSARY TO ENTER OR WIN.
Void wherever prohibited or restricted by law.

Limit one entry per person for the Sweepstakes period. Not responsible for: late, lost, stolen, damaged, undelivered, mutilated, illegible, or misdirected entries; postage due; or typographical errors in the rules. Entries void if they are in whole or in part illegible, incomplete, or damaged. No facsimiles, mechanical reproductions or forged entries. Sweepstakes starts on May 1, 2004 and all entries must be postmarked January 15, 2005, and received by January 21, 2005 (the "Sweepstakes period").

All entries become the property of Simon & Schuster Inc. and will not be acknowledged or returned.

Simon & Schuster Inc. will choose one (1) winner in a random drawing consisting of all eligible entries received, and will award one (1) Grand Prize to an eligible U.S. or Canadian entrant.

Grand Prize Winners will be eligible for a chance for a walk-on role on the NBC Series "American Dreams" (the "Series"). All details of the walk-on role to be determined by Sponsors, in Sponsors' sole discretion, subject to availability and production exigencies. Winners must be available during the Series' production schedule and on the dates selected by Sponsors. Grand Prize includes round-trip coach air transportation for 4 (at least one person must be 18 years or older) from a major airport nearest the winner's residence to Los Angeles, CA, hotel accommodations in Los Angeles (2 standard rooms, double occupancy) for 3 days and 2 nights, ground transportation to and from the airport to the hotel, and a visit to the NBC set of the television series "*American Dreams*," provided that the show is in production during winner's trip. Prize does not include transfers, gratuities, upgrades, personal incidentals, meals or any other any expenses not specified or listed herein. Total retail value of Grand Prize: approximately $4,000. All travel subject to availability. Restrictions and blackout dates may apply. Sponsors reserve the right to substitute a similar prize of equal or greater value at their sole discretion. Travel and hotel arrangements to be determined by the Sponsors. The Sponsors in their sole discretion reserve the right to provide ground transportation in lieu of air transportation.

One (1) Grand Prize winner will be selected at random from all eligible entries received in a drawing to be held on or about January 22, 2005. Winner will be allowed to choose 3 people to accompany him/her on the Grand Prize trip, at least one travel companion must be the winner's parent or legal guardian. Any other minor travel companions must also be accompanied by their parent or legal guardian. The Grand Prize winner must be able to travel during the months of February 2005 through April 2005. If the Grand Prize winner is unable to travel on the dates specified by the Sponsors, then prize will be forfeited and awarded to an alternate winner. In the event that the show *American Dreams* is cancelled, postponed or delayed for any reason, or if any prize component is not available for any reason, then Sponsors will only be responsible for awarding the remaining elements of the prize which constitute full satisfaction of the Sponsors prize obligation to winner & no substitute or additional compensation will be awarded. Winner will be notified by U.S. mail and by telephone, within 15 days of the random drawing. Any notification/prize that is returned as undeliverable will result in an alternate winner being chosen. Odds of winning depend on the number of eligible entries received. Sweepstakes is open to legal residents of the continental U.S. (excluding Alaska, Hawaii, Puerto Rico, and Guam) and Canada (excluding Quebec) ages 8-16 as of March 1, 2004. Proof of age is required to claim prize. If winner is a minor, then prizes will be awarded in the name of the winner's parent or legal guardian. Void wherever prohibited or restricted by law. All provincial, federal, state, and local laws apply. Employees of Simon & Schuster Inc., National Broadcasting Company, Inc., ("NBC") (collectively, the "Sponsors") and their respective suppliers, parent companies, subsidiaries, affiliates, agencies, and participating retailers, and persons connected with the use, marketing, or conducting of this Sweepstakes are not eligible. Family members living in the same household as any of the individuals referred to in the preceding sentence are not eligible. Prizes are not transferable, may not be redeemed for cash, and may not be substituted except by Sponsors, in which case a prize of equal or greater value will be awarded. If the prize is forfeited or unclaimed, if a prize notification is undeliverable, or in the event of noncompliance with any of these requirements, the prize will be forfeited and the Sponsors will randomly select from remaining eligible entries an alternate winner.

If the potential winner is a Canadian resident, then he/she must correctly answer a skill-based question administered by mail. If the potential winner does not correctly answer the skill-based question, then an alternate winner will be selected from all remaining eligible entries.

All expenses on receipt and use of prizes including provincial, federal, state, and local taxes are the sole responsibility of the of the winner's parent or legal guardian. On winner's behalf, winner's parents or legal guardians will be required to execute and return an Affidavit of Eligibility and a Liability/Publicity Release and all other legal documents that the Sweepstakes Sponsors may require (including a W-9 tax form) within 15 days of attempted notification or an alternate winner may be selected. Each travel companion or travel companion's parent or legal guardian if travel companion is a minor, will be required to execute a liability release form prior to ticketing.

By participating in the Sweepstakes, entrants agree to be bound by these rules and the decisions of the judges and Sponsors, which are final in all matters relating to this Sweepstakes. Failure to comply with these Official Rules may result in disqualification of your entry and prohibition of any further participation in this Sweepstakes. By accepting the prize, the winner's parent or legal guardian grants to Sponsors the right to use his/her name and likeness for any advertising, promotional, trade, or any other purpose without further compensation or permission, except where prohibited by law.

By entering, entrants waive Sponsors and their respective divisions, subsidiaries, affiliates, advertising, production, and promotion agencies from any and all liability for any loss, harm, damages, costs, or expenses, including without limitation property damages, personal injury, and/or death, arising out of participation in the Sweepstakes, the acceptance, possession, use, or misuse of any prize, claims based on publicity rights, rights of privacy, intellectual property rights, defamation, or merchandise delivery.

For the name of the prize winner (available after February 5, 2005) send a separate, stamped, self-addressed envelope to Winners' List, Dreams Come True Sweepstakes, Simon & Schuster Children's Marketing Department, 1230 Avenue of the Americas, New York, New York 10020.

Sponsors: Simon & Schuster Children's Publishing, 1230 Avenue of the Americas, New York, NY 10020; and National Broadcasting Company, Inc., 3400 West Olive Avenue #600, Burbank, CA 91505.